WAITING FOR THEM

SPARKS IN TEXAS, BOOK 4

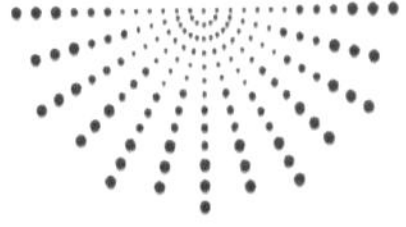

MARI CARR

Something so wrong never felt so right.

When Harley returns home, her bandmates, Caleb and Tyson, are there waiting for her. Shortly after her brother's death, they made a mistake. One that haunts them and keeps them up all night, tossing and turning–with desire.

Harley left Texas to figure out these new feelings she has for Ty and Cal. There is nothing on earth more precious to her than their friendship. So why is she suddenly imagining doing a Texas three-step with them?

Unwilling to wait for them any longer, Harley's ready for an adventure. And it includes love, laughter, skinny-dipping, bluegrass and the two men who make her heart dance.

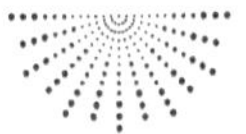

CHAPTER ONE

"**W**ell, look what the cat dragged in."

Harley Mills grinned as she got out of her car. "Hey, Eugene. Good to see you." She walked around the car as Eugene uncapped the gas tank and started to pump. After a year in Florida, she was used to pumping her own gas. However, in Maris, Texas, the one-pump town came complete with Eugene Barton, who believed in full service only. Mainly because—like his mother, Phyllis—he loved to talk.

"You back to stay?"

She nodded as she gestured to the backseat of her car, loaded with boxes. She wasn't sure how she'd managed to acquire so much crap in just twelve months, but somewhere along the line, shopping had become therapy.

Eugene finished filling her tank, washed her windshield and thanked her for the cash. She had come prepared. Eugene could do credit, but it took him some time—typically a lot of time—to run it through the machine. Harley was anxious to get back to the farm.

She was saved from further conversation when a phone inside the station started ringing.

"Welcome home!" Eugene shouted as he hustled inside to grab the phone.

Home.

Harley smiled. When she crawled out of Maris last year, she'd been a broken girl, and in her distraught mind, she had wondered if she would ever come back. However, time had a way of healing all wounds, and now she was pretty sure she'd never leave again.

* * *

"HEY, Eugene. I'm making pot roast for dinner. You planning on stopping by?"

Eugene rolled his eyes, grateful his mama couldn't see him. She'd whack him on the head if she saw him being disrespectful to her. But damn, why did she feel the need to call him every blessed afternoon? He never ate anywhere but her house for dinner, and hadn't in twenty-eight years. She knew that.

"Yeah, Mama. Closing up here at six. Be there by six-fifteen."

"Good. Can you stop on the way and pick up some bread from the bakery? I got a hankering for some sourdough. Beverly Sparks makes the best."

"I'll grab a loaf for you. Speaking of...guess who's back in town?" The quickest way to get off the phone with his mother was to feed her gossip. She wouldn't waste words on *him* if she thought she had the scoop on something no one else knew.

"Who?"

"Harley Mills."

"No! Really?"

"Just filled up her tank."

"She back to stay?"

"Says she is."

"Hmmm." His mother digested that information and then did exactly what he expected. "Well, I gotta go. Don't forget the bread."

Mama disconnected the phone before Eugene could say goodbye.

BEVERLY WIPED her hands on her apron when the phone started ringing and smacked her brother-in-law's hand when he reached for another fresh-from-the-oven chocolate chip cookie. "Dammit, TJ. You're gonna eat me out of business. Go back to work."

TJ grinned sheepishly but didn't bother to move. Instead, he remained where he was, his eyes glued to the tray, letting her know he would simply wait for another opportunity to grab a second cookie when she wasn't expecting it.

"Louise!" she called out across the shop. "Control your husband." She would let her sister-in-law deal with TJ. She picked up the phone on the third ring. "Sparks Bakery."

Beverly closed her eyes, instantly sorry she had answered the phone when she heard Phyllis Barton's voice. The woman wore her out. Constantly telling tales or, in lieu of anything juicy, complaining about whatever aches and pains she was feeling that day.

"Oh, hey, Phyllis. How are you?"

"You hear who's back in town?"

Despite the part of her that knew gossiping was bad, Beverly's interest was instantly piqued. "No. Who?"

"Harley," Phyllis replied.

"Really? Are you sure?" Beverly asked.

"Is she sure about what?" TJ leaned closer, trying to listen to her conversation. The man was the biggest busybody in town, and he'd no doubt heard her say Phyllis' name. TJ knew that if he had any serious competition for being Maris' most shameless gossip, it was Phyllis.

"Shh, TJ," she admonished as Phyllis explained how Eugene had filled up Harley's tank and how she had told him she was moving back home.

"Well, isn't that something?" Beverly replied.

"Isn't *what* something?" TJ asked impatiently.

She waved him away and then assured Phyllis she would hold back a loaf of sourdough for her. "I'll have it ready for Eugene when he gets here," she promised before saying goodbye.

When she hung up, TJ was still standing next to her.

"Well?" he asked.

Beverly chuckled. "I'll tell you the gossip if you promise to keep your grubby paws out of my cookies and go back to work."

"If you give me something juicy, I'll have a *reason* to go back to work."

Beverly thought—as she always did—how lucky TJ was to have the girls. He may own Sparks Barbeque, but it was the Sparks' girls who kept it running and thriving.

"Harley is back in town."

TJ's eyes lit up as if he'd just won the Powerball. "I gotta go." He turned toward the door—but quickly snatched two more chocolate chip cookies off the tray before hustling out.

"Thomas Junior! You scamp!" Beverly called out as Louise shook her head, not at her husband, but at Beverly.

"You should have known better, Bev," Louise said as the door closed behind TJ.

Yeah, Beverly thought. *I should have.*

* * *

Her dad strolled into the restaurant, wiping the last remnants of chocolate from the corners of his lips.

"Aunt Bev is going to start locking you out of that bakery if you don't stop stealing her cookies. Was that batch for us?" Macie asked.

Sparks Bakery didn't just operate their own little sales counter; they also supplied all the desserts sold at the restaurant next door. But her dad had a way of eating more than his fair share from both places.

"Naw," Dad said. "That batch was going in the display case. And I only stole three."

Macie topped up the bourbon she'd just poured with a splash of Coke and handed it to her cousin, Gia, to deliver to Roger Millhouse.

"Only three?" Macie added, continuing the conversation with her dad. "You must be losing your touch."

"Needed to get back here. I have some news."

Macie tried to act impassive, but failed to dim her interest quick enough. Dad grinned, pleased to have sparked her curiosity. Now he'd make her beg for whatever juicy tidbit he claimed to have.

"Oh yeah?" She adopted a casual, bored tone that fooled no one.

"You got some gossip?" Earl asked from his perch at the bar. If Macie could have reached, she would have whacked him on the back of the head.

Never show interest.

That was rule number one with TJ Sparks. If you did, he'd keep you hanging on for hours, simply because he got a kick out of it.

Her dad rubbed his hands together. "That I do. Just learned something *very* interesting."

"What's that?" Coop asked.

Macie sighed. *Et tu, Brute?*

Hank Cooper, a regular at the restaurant since his wife's death, should have known better too. He'd been here plenty enough to know how this shit would go down.

"Coop," she muttered softly.

Coop looked at her, and then chuckled when he realized what he'd done. "There's something wrong with your family, sweetheart."

She didn't take offense. She'd known that since the cradle. "Tell me something I don't know. And strap yourself in. It's gonna be a long night."

Her dad continued to hem and haw, teasing them as his news evolved from something merely of interest to the biggest thing to happen in Maris in months, maybe years. Somewhere along the line, her father's cronies had convinced TJ to play Twenty Questions as a way of making the revelation.

That was when Macie lost it. "Good God Almighty. Don't you fellas have anything better to do with your time than to sit in this restaurant, drink beer and tell tales? Don't your wives want you at home? Don't you want to *be* with them?"

The matching looks of horror on the faces of no less than six older retired men answered her question.

Regardless, old man Baxter put it into words. "Good Lord, no. Sparks Barbeque is the reason I'm celebrating my sixtieth anniversary next month. Me and the missus would have split up ages ago if I hadn't had this oasis to come to."

Macie laughed loudly. "Jesus. Oasis! This place?"

It wasn't that she disagreed with the assessment. In her mind, there wasn't anywhere better on earth than her little spot behind this bar, surrounded by family and friends. Unless, of course, it was Vegas. But she didn't want to live there. Just see it.

Secretly, she was pleased Baxter loved it as much as she did, and she certainly approved of his description.

The men ignored her outburst and began their game.

"Is the gossip about a male or female?" Earl asked.

"Only yes/no questions," TJ corrected as the men took turns throwing questions at him.

"Is it about a man?"

TJ shook his head.

"Female?"

He nodded as Macie rolled her eyes. "If it's not about a male, I think we can assume female, jackass. Way to waste a question."

Coop chuckled. "Thought you didn't want to play the game."

"Shut up, Coop."

"Somebody having an affair?" Baxter asked.

"No."

"Somebody movin' away?"

Dad tilted his head. "No, but that's close."

"Someone movin' back?" Coop asked. Macie lifted her eyebrows at him, but Coop just shrugged and gave her a sheepish grin. "Sorry. Got carried away."

"Yes," Dad confirmed.

A woman moving back?

Macie had the answer in an instant. And she agreed with her dad. It *was* big news. "Harley."

Her dad sighed and leaned back against his chair. "Dammit, Macie! You're not supposed to blurt out the answer like that."

She snorted. "Actually, I'm pretty sure you are. That's the whole point of the game."

"What about Harley?" Adele asked, lugging a tray full of food into the dining room from the kitchen.

Macie grinned at her sister. "Apparently, she's back in town."

"Harley's back?" Paige said, following Adele into the dining room. It was as if there was some sort of Bat signal that went up whenever someone had something interesting to tell in Maris. Macie didn't have a clue how everyone knew, but it felt to her as if more and more people were just suddenly showing up as word of Harley's return spread.

Unfortunately, despite the sudden influx, the two people Macie wanted to see the most right now hadn't arrived. Regardless, she kept one eye on the door. They'd be here soon enough—and she'd tackle her dad if she had to, to be the first one to give them the news.

* * *

TYSON HADN'T MADE it three steps into Sparks Barbeque before he was hit with Macie's question.

"You hear who's back in town?"

He wasn't sure what the answer was, but when every head in the place turned in his direction, it was apparent the good people of Maris were anxious to hear his response.

He shook his head as he approached the bar and claimed a stool next to Chas and one of the guys who worked on his construction crew. From the looks of it, both men had just gotten off work. He smiled and nodded an unspoken hello.

"Nope, Mace. Been at the hospital in Douglas all day, checking on a few patients."

Macie grinned, and then poured him a draft. Without answering her own question. Damn woman loved drawing out suspense. She'd gotten the annoying habit from her father, who was Tyson's Uncle TJ.

It drove him nuts when they played this game. Always had.

He took a sip of his beer, pretending he couldn't care less who'd decided to return to their tiny two-horse town. In truth, he was dog-tired and really wasn't particularly interested in whatever scrap of gossip she had to spread. "What's the special tonight?"

She scowled and pursed her lips. "You're not even a little bit curious?"

He shrugged. "Macie, there are a lot of folks who've made it out of this town. I can't even begin to venture a guess as to which one decided to come back."

"Harley," Macie said.

Tyson fought to keep his expression blank. Too many eyes

were still pointed in his direction, including Uncle TJ's, as he walked into the dining room from the kitchen. The look on his uncle's face told him TJ was pissed he'd missed the opportunity to break the news himself.

"Really?" Tyson asked, trying to adopt a nonchalant tone, but he failed. It came out too anxious.

"Yeah. Eugene filled her tank at the gas station. Said she told him she was back to stay."

Tyson was supposed to meet Caleb here for dinner. They shared a house on the lake, but the cupboards were bare this week. Neither one of them had had time to hit the grocery store. As such, they'd decided to just hit the restaurant for supper. Groceries would be tomorrow's problem. Since his dad's heart attack, Caleb had been pulling longer hours at the Feed and Seed, and as one of only two general practitioners in town, Tyson had learned shortly after opening up shop that illnesses and accidents never took a holiday.

Paige walked into the room from her office. His younger sister had no ability for cooking or bartending and, according to his cousins, her waitressing skills left something to be desired as well. However, she was the best math student to ever graduate from Maris High School and she had a knack for business. As such, TJ had declared her office manager, putting her in charge of the books, ordering, scheduling and everything else he hated to do that resembled paperwork.

She made a beeline for him. "Hey, big brother."

Tyson gave her a quick hug. "Hiya, munchkin."

"Macie tell you Harley was back in town?"

He nodded. "Yeah, she did."

"You didn't know she was coming home?"

"No, Paige. You know I haven't talked to her in a year." And he'd missed her like crazy every single second of it.

"I know. I was thinking maybe she called to give you a heads-up. I mean, y'all are *only* best friends."

Tyson didn't blame Harley for keeping her return to Texas a secret. When she'd left, her life had been in total turmoil, something he'd inadvertently added to. It wasn't like they'd parted on bad terms. She had simply asked him and Caleb for time, and they had given it to her because they knew she needed it. Desperately.

"You going to see her?" Paige asked.

He nodded. "Yeah. I am." Tyson stood, realizing he didn't give a shit what anyone thought of his hasty exit. Harley was back in town and he was going to go see her. Let TJ and his cronies make of that what they would.

"Listen, Mace. Put the beer on my tab."

Macie smiled and gave him a wink. He absentmindedly waved goodbye to a few folks as he dug his cell out of his back pocket. Tapping the number, he waited for Caleb to answer.

"Change of plans, Cal. I'm going to swing by the store to pick you up. Our girl is back in town."

CHAPTER TWO

$\mathcal{H}$arley climbed out of her car and sucked in a deep breath of Texas' humid air. While it wasn't all that much different from the mugginess of Florida, to her, it felt unique. Special.

This dusty old farm smelled like home, and she was so glad to be back.

She glanced up when the screen door slammed, and she dropped the suitcase she'd just tugged out of the backseat. Sprinting toward the front porch, she launched herself into her beloved granddad's arms.

He was there—ready and waiting for her. He squeezed her just tight enough to take her breath away for a moment, and she soaked up his strength and the scent of his pipe tobacco. Granddad was seventy-five, but the man could easily pass for sixty. He was built like a bull, big, lean, and muscular. His head was completely bald, but given the fact he wore a big-ass Stetson 24/7, it was easy to forget that fact. Folks around town liked to joke that old Willie Mills probably slept in that big white hat of his.

"There's my girl. Damn, it's good to have you home."

He released her and took a step back, studying her appearance. "You look good. Healthy. Happy."

She smiled. "I feel…a lot better. You were right to tell me to get away."

"I think my exact words were 'Get the hell outta this town before it kills you.'"

At the time, Harley hadn't really wanted to go. Maris and this farm were all she'd ever known. Unlike her best friends, Caleb and Tyson, she hadn't gone away to college, hadn't ever seen much more of the world than the occasional treks to Dallas with her brother, Johnnie, to see medical specialists. "Aunt Ginny sends her love."

Harley had spent the past year with Granddad's sister, Genevieve, in St. Pete Beach, Florida. She would be forever grateful to the kind woman for opening her home to her when she needed somewhere to escape. On top of that, Aunt Ginny had given her a job at a little boutique she owned on the strip. Twelve months of long walks on the beach, the atmosphere that of an eternal holiday, and the opportunity to disappear inside herself for a little while had healed so many wounds.

Aunt Ginny would have let her stay forever. In fact, if she'd had her way, Harley would have moved in permanently and the store would have been her inheritance. Her beloved great aunt had thrown that little nugget out there to tempt her, but Harley had woken up two weeks ago and known it was time to come home.

"Did you talk her into coming back for a visit?"

Harley shook her head with a grin. Aunt Ginny and Granddad adored each other, but they were both as stubborn as the day was long. Granddad refused to leave the farm, claiming there was too much work to do, and Ginny insisted it would be the height of foolishness for her to travel to Texas on vacation when she had the ocean right outside her front door.

"Nope, but she wanted me to pass along that open invitation to Florida again. Not that either one of us ever expect you to take a vacation."

Granddad gestured around at the farm. "Too much work to be done here."

"Not with *me* back now. We can split the duties in half."

Granddad rubbed his chin and glanced back toward the front door. "Yeah. About that, Harl—"

"Harley?"

Harley frowned when her dad walked out onto the front porch.

"What are you doing here?" Her tone was far from friendly.

Damn. She'd told herself she had the bitterness under control, but she also hadn't expected to see her father walking out of *her* home, barefoot and drinking a glass of iced tea.

"I..." Her dad stumbled in the face of her fury. She tried to batten it down, to put it away. That was why she'd left. So she could move away from the anger that consumed her.

"He lives here." Granddad supplied the answer, and Harley felt as if all the air had just been punched out of her.

"What?"

"Moved back in about eight months ago."

Harley was numb with shock. "But—"

Her dad took a step closer. "I'm sober, Harley."

She rolled her eyes. "Oh yeah. Because I haven't heard *those* words a million times."

"Harley," Granddad said gruffly.

She turned to him. "Granddad, we've been here so many times before! I thought..." She tried to pull in a deep breath, but the air was suddenly too thick. It wasn't just Harley who was hurt every time her dad fell off the wagon. Her granddad suffered as well. "It's just—"

Granddad's stern expression softened a bit. "I'm gonna have to ask you to trust me on this one, baby girl."

Though she hated to admit it to herself, the fact that her dad was here sort of made the conversation she'd hoped to have with her granddad later a bit easier. She'd been struggling with a decision during the entire eighteen-hour drive from Florida. Part of the appeal of living in Florida was that for the first time in her life, she'd been out in the real world, on her own—more or less. After all, Aunt Ginny had a huge group of friends and was active in two book clubs, a knitting circle and took line-dancing classes two nights a week.

Finding out that her dad was living and working on the farm made it easier for her to tell her grandfather she was thinking of looking for a roommate and moving into town.

"Okay." She would drop the discussion of her father's so-called sobriety for now. She turned back toward her car. "I need to get my stuff."

"Need help?" her dad offered.

"No," she replied without looking at him. "I've got it."

Granddad sighed heavily, as if he were disappointed in her. The idea made her feel guilty and furious at the same time. No doubt her granddad had had some higher hopes for her homecoming. Problem was, he was way better at forgive-ness—and second, third, fortieth chances—than she was.

She retrieved the suitcase she'd dropped by the side of her car, slung her bathroom bag over her arm and grabbed her battered banjo case. There were several other boxes in the backseat, but they could wait until later.

When she returned to the porch, her dad had gone back inside. Granddad reached out and cupped her cheek. "I missed you so damn much, kid."

She had missed him too. Missed this dusty old farmhouse, the light, lingering smell of manure and the perfect silence. She had adored the constant white noise of the waves crashing on the shore, but Harley enjoyed the quiet peace of this farm just as much.

"I'll put a pot of chili on for supper. And I'll be sure to double the recipe," Granddad said.

She laughed. "I don't eat that much."

"Not worrying about you. Figure those boys won't wait five minutes to head out here when they realize you're back."

Harley forced a smile, though there was a part of her that feared neither Caleb nor Tyson would show up. Not after the way she'd run. After all, it hadn't just been Johnnie's death or the shit at home she'd tried to escape. She'd left *them* as well.

Told them she needed a clean break, which meant no phone calls, emails. Nothing. Radio silence for twelve months. It was the longest the three of them had ever gone without speaking to each other. She'd hated every minute of it, but she hadn't reached out to them. And they hadn't attempted to contact her either.

Of course, she'd asked them not to. Even so, part of her thought maybe they'd find that request impossible and they'd go against their word. Not that she blamed them for remaining quiet. While they hadn't separated on bad terms, they'd definitely parted on bizarre, OMG, WTF terms. It had taken her most of the year away to wrap her head around their last time together. To process what had happened and to try to figure out what came next.

"I'm not so sure about that."

Granddad held the screen door open. "I am. Your room's all ready for you. Clean sheets and all."

She thanked him, feeling slightly guilty as she watched him head for the kitchen. She wasn't sure he'd like the idea of her moving out so soon after returning home.

Looking around the front foyer, she didn't know where her father had gone. He'd probably found somewhere to hide. She was grateful he was keeping his distance and letting her get used to the idea he was here. For a split second, she let that kindness inspire hope, but experience had taught her to smother those embers before they turned to flame.

She paused when she reached the foot of the stairs and glanced toward the closed door of the room on the right.

Johnnie's room.

The constant ache that never really left her flared up a bit at the sight of that door, at the realization he wasn't there anymore. If there was one thing she knew for certain, it was that Johnnie would not have wanted her to mourn him as long as she had.

She missed him every second of every day, but she'd noticed more and more that when the memories returned, she could let them come without tears following. She had finally reached a place where she could think of her brother and smile. Once that corner was turned, she had known it was time to come home.

Aunt Ginny had spent the better part of her time in Florida convincing Harley to move on, to live her life to the fullest, to have enough adventures for her and Johnnie both.

Harley climbed the stairs, a spring in her step, as she considered taking her aunt's advice. After so many years of standing still, she was pretty sure she wouldn't mind an adventure or two. If only she could figure out how.

As she entered her bedroom, Harley turned, taking in the lifetime of mementoes she had accumulated. She had lived in this house since she was born.

She always imagined her life in two parts. There was the time before Johnnie's accident, when she'd shared this house with her granddad, parents and brother. That was the hazy part, the one she struggled to remember.

Then there was the time after. That part she remembered in all its painful clarity. She recalled her mother's inability to deal with anything, her father's dissent into the bottle, and the sound of Johnnie's ventilator.

Harley forced those memories away. She closed her eyes and took a deep breath. She'd spent too much time getting herself to a place where she could handle this. There would be no backtracking.

Opening her suitcase, she debated returning her clothes to their usual drawers, and then closed the lid again. It was silly. She didn't have anywhere else to go, but she knew it was time for her to leave the farm and find a place of her own in Maris. Unpacking felt fruitless, now that she had made her decision to live elsewhere. Of course, she didn't fancy the idea of living out of a suitcase for however many weeks it took her to find a place, either. She was going to have to put her crap away. But that could wait until after dinner.

She'd just finished placing some of her toiletries on the shelf in the bathroom, brushing her teeth and washing her face to freshen up, when her granddad called for her.

"Dinner can't be ready this quick," she said as she walked to the top of the stairs.

Granddad didn't reply. Instead, he gave her a shit-eating grin as he gestured toward Caleb and Tyson, standing next to him.

They looked more handsome than ever, and her heart leapt as she dashed down the steps and launched herself into Tyson's arms. He was ready for her, hugging her tightly as they all laughed. When he released her, it was Caleb's turn to welcome her home. He was a big, burly teddy bear of a man, and the second she was in his arms, he picked her up and spun her around until she was dizzy.

"Put me down, you idiot! Let me look at you guys."

Caleb set her back on her feet and she took a step away. "Is that gray hair, Tyson?"

He reached up and lightly touched his sideburns. "Seriously? That's the first thing you notice? I've been hitting the gym like a champ." He flexed his arm muscles. "Check out that gun show."

Caleb snorted. "Jesus. We've been in the house three seconds and you're already showing off the fact you got one new little muscle. He's been impossible to live with since that thing appeared. Now, if you want to see a gun show..."

Tyson and Harley joked that Caleb had been born with muscles. It probably helped that he'd been helping out at his dad's Feed and Seed since he'd learned to walk. Lugging around fifty-pound bags of oats and barley and big-ass hay bales had ensured Caleb was a walking, talking bulldozer of a man. All through middle school, they'd called him Thor until he'd put his foot down and told them he wasn't going to be stuck with that nickname for life.

In Maris, playful names had a tendency to stick, and that wasn't always a good thing. As Stinky Matthews, Tiny Partlow and Rat Jenkins could attest to.

"You boys never change," her granddad said, slapping Tyson on the back. "Always trying to impress the girls. You staying for dinner? Got a pot of chili on the stove."

"And cornbread?" Caleb asked.

Granddad scowled. "Is there any other way to eat chili?"

Caleb rubbed his hands together with glee. "Damn. I'm glad you finally decided to get your ass home, Harl. I've missed your granddad's cooking."

Harley raised her hand. "And there you have it, Granddad. The proof I've been looking for that confirms Ty and Cal are only friends with me because you feed them. Bit like encouraging stray cats to keep coming back."

Granddad shook his head. "I know better than that. You two bring your instruments?"

"Would we show up here without them?" Tyson asked, imitating Granddad's affronted tone after the cornbread question.

Harley was delighted by his response. Not that she'd expected them to come here empty-handed. Of everything she'd missed while she was away—her bedroom, her granddad and her friends—the thing she'd missed most was making music with these guys.

"Logan coming by later?" Granddad asked.

Tyson shrugged. "To be honest, we didn't call him. He's...a bit preoccupied these days."

Harley tilted her head curiously. "Did he get back with Jane?" Logan had been dating his girlfriend, Jane, for several years, but they'd broken up shortly before Johnnie's death. Harley had never felt like the match was a very good fit.

"Nah. They're still broken up," Caleb replied.

"Oh." Harley gave them a wicked grin. "So he's got himself a new girlfriend. Guess that means he's spending all his time in the bedroom these days. He's probably in all-out horn-dog mode after so many years with boring Jane. This poor new girl will be getting a workout...without the gym."

Caleb glanced at Tyson as he spoke. "Easy, Harley. Might not want to go too far with the sex jokes this time around."

Harley laughed. "Oh my God! For real? Which one of your cousins is he hooking up with?"

Tyson scowled. "Lacy."

Her eyes widened. "And Evan hasn't killed him yet?" Lacy's brother, Evan, was part of Maris' tiny police force, and very protective of his sister and female cousins.

"He punched him once, but so far Logan is being a gentleman."

Harley tilted her head, but Tyson didn't let her say what she was thinking. He didn't have to. Logan might be a gentleman in public, but the guy played a little rougher in the bedroom, and they knew it.

There were no secrets between any of them in the band. They'd formed Ty's Collective their sophomore year in high school, becoming as close as siblings. Harley participated in their locker-room conversations as if she were one of the guys, which was how they had always treated her.

None of them were shy about sharing the racier details of their affairs, and between the four of them, they'd all had their share of casual relationships and one-night stands.

Even when Tyson and Caleb went off to college, whenever they were home on breaks, the four of them fell back together, picking up their instruments and playing as if they'd never been apart. The group was solid. Tight. The best of friends.

Tyson crossed his arms, drawing her attention once again to *the guns*. The man wasn't kidding. He had gotten into serious shape while she was away. "We don't talk about Logan's sex life with my cousin."

She grinned wickedly. "That's a shame. Knowing Logan, I bet there are some pretty racy, kinky, wild stories to—"

The rest of her jest didn't land, as Tyson grabbed her in a headlock and messed up her hair. She giggled as she tried to get loose. Horseplay had been a part of their friendship since they were kids. Harley kept thinking that eventually they'd get too old for such silliness, but that day hadn't shown up yet.

Granddad shook his head again at their antics. "I'll let y'all catch up while I finish dinner. Make sure you figure out a day for a barn party. And make it soon. I've been missing those things."

"I just got home," Harley called out to her granddad's retreating back.

Granddad didn't bother to turn around as he walked into the kitchen. "Just do it."

Caleb wrapped his arm around Harley's shoulders and walked with her to the living room as Tyson followed. "Not gonna lie. I like the idea of a barn party a lot."

She did too. They'd held a bunch of barn parties on her

granddad's farm over the years. So many that Granddad had actually built a second barn about ten years earlier that he used for farm work, leaving the stage and dance floor set up in the original one for their performances.

Harley sank down on the couch. Caleb grabbed the other end, while Tyson took the chair next to her. "Maybe we should hammer out a few numbers to see if we can still play together."

Tyson shook his head. "We've taken hiatuses in the past and it's never been a problem for us to start back up."

"Yeah, but we never took this much time off. Even when you guys were away at college, we made time to play over the breaks." Harley regretted drawing attention to how long she'd been gone.

"You're back to stay, right?" Caleb asked. "No more running off?"

She narrowed her eyes, pretending to be angry. "I wasn't running."

Tyson, the most compassionate man on the planet, leaned closer and grasped her hand. "We know that," he said, flashing Caleb a warning glance. "You needed time to mourn, to get yourself together."

Harley had known coming back would be rough. It was one of the reasons she'd put it off longer than she should have. After Johnnie died, she fell apart. Rather than deal with all the stuff piling up on her, she'd cut and run—with Granddad's blessing.

"I'm better now, Ty. Honest."

He studied her face intently for a few moments and then his smile grew. "Yeah. I'd say you look ready to take on the world. You lose weight?"

"I've started running."

"Running?" Caleb asked, not bothering to hide his surprise. "Thought you said the only way you'd take up running was if someone was chasing you with a knife."

Tyson shook his head. "Actually, I think she revised that plan. Said she'd just lie down and play dead instead."

"Very funny, assholes," she said, loving how easy it was to be back with them. After the way things had ended, she worried it wouldn't be this simple to put the pieces back together. Of course, they still had a lot of stuff to talk about, but she was grateful they'd shown up, that they were giving her a chance to set things right.

She appreciated Tyson's encouragement as she glanced over her shoulder toward the front hallway. "Did you know my dad moved back in here?"

Tyson nodded and Caleb shrugged, explaining, "It's Maris, honey. Man can't take a dump in the woods without twelve people discussing it."

"Crude, Cal. But accurate." She sighed. "I just can't understand why Granddad would let him come back after—"

"You've been gone a year," Tyson said, cutting her off. "Some things have changed."

Harley hated the part of her that hoped that was true. But she refused to get her hopes up, only to have them dashed by her dad again. Part of her reason for leaving Maris was because she needed to get away from the train wreck that was her folks.

"I'm glad you're back," Tyson said, still holding her hand.

Then Caleb reached over and put a comforting hand on her shoulder. And just like that, everything in her world seemed to fall right back into place. The times she was the strongest, the happiest, the most secure, were these moments. When it was just the three of them.

Then before she could stop them from coming, the memories of the week Johnnie died crashed over her, assaulting her, taking her down. She'd done some crazy, irrational things, like running away.

Like kissing Tyson and Caleb. Together. In the barn.

The memory of those kisses had woven themselves around every aspect of her life while she was away, keeping her up at night, distracted during the day, and so hot and bothered, it was a physical ache that never left her.

Her entire life had changed the week Johnnie passed away, and the time away hadn't altered any of it.

Granddad still made chili once a week. Maris was still filled with busybodies and gossips. Her parents were, most likely, still fucked up. Johnnie was still gone.

And she was still completely in love with *both* of her best friends.

CHAPTER THREE

Tyson kicked back in the Adirondack chair, resting his feet on the ledge of the fire pit as he took a sip of coffee. The sun was just peeking out behind the trees on the other side of the lake. It wasn't quite seven yet. He'd always been an early bird, but that habit grew when he bought this house on the lake. There was nothing like the crisp morning air or the gentle lapping of the water against the dock to start the morning off right. It soothed his soul, helped him get grounded, ready.

Except for today.

He and Caleb had stayed at Harley's until nearly eleven. They'd plowed through a huge pot of chili with her dad and granddad. Logan and Lacy showed up in time for dessert after a quick text from Harley, inviting them out.

Then they had retired to the living room, where they'd fired up the instruments and played through every single one of their favorites. Her granddad made three phone calls to start the Maris chain and before they knew it, they were locked into doing a performance in the barn a week from

Saturday. Before Tyson had made it home last night, he'd gotten no less than ten texts—most from his cousins, all promising to be there.

So he should be on top of the world this morning. Harley was home. The band was back together. He was going to spend next Saturday night doing his favorite thing—jamming out onstage, getting lost in the music, surrounded by the people he loved most.

Instead, he felt like a man living at the base of a volcano and the lava was sliding toward him. He hadn't had a chance to talk to Harley alone last night, to try to set things right after the last time they'd seen each other.

He should have started the conversation when it had just been her, Caleb and him in the living room, but it didn't feel right to launch into it five minutes after she'd gotten back into town. Plus, he thought it might be easier to discuss without Caleb around, though that would definitely piss his friend off. The two of them had made this mess together, so they should straighten it out that way, too.

However, he and Caleb hadn't really discussed that day since Harley's departure, either. It was as if they'd tacitly agreed to simply let the subject drop until her return. Which had been stupid and shortsighted, but certainly safer. Now she was back, and he had tossed and turned all night, his mind racing over what the hell would happen now.

He and his best friend had acted on instinct, on impulse, and kissed Harley just four days after Johnnie's funeral.

Harley had been devastated by the loss of her beloved brother, and neither he nor Caleb could stand seeing her so upset. So they'd gone to see her...

. . .

HARLEY'S GRANDDAD met them on the front porch when they climbed out of the car. He pointed toward the barn. "She said she was going to check on the horses about an hour ago."

Tyson and Caleb knew there was precious little checking to be done. No doubt she'd wanted to be alone. They hesitated briefly before Mr. Mills waved his hand at them. "Go on and find her. See if she's okay. I was about to do that very thing myself, but I'm sure she'd rather see you two."

The older man stepped back into the house, so Tyson and Caleb headed for the barn. She was sitting in the far corner on a square bale of hay. Her eyes were puffy and red, betraying the fact she'd been crying. However, it appeared her sorrow had waned for the time being and now she just sat alone in the quiet, with a distant expression on her face.

They were halfway to her before she even noticed them. And then, in true Harley fashion, she dug deep for a friendly smile that looked like it threatened to crack her face. The damn woman was a master at hiding her sadness, at painting on cheerful expressions despite her misery.

Tyson hated that she felt like she had to hide her grief from them. She had been stoic throughout everything. Holding on to her composure when Johnnie fell ill and was rushed to the hospital, when he was taken off the ventilator and his heart stopped beating. She sat next to her granddad and planned the funeral without falling apart, taking care of all the things her parents were too weak to handle. She had spoken at the funeral with poise and grace, offering the most touching eulogy Tyson had ever heard.

There'd only been one dry eye in the place when she'd finished—hers.

"Hey." Her voice was thick, hoarse. She'd obviously had a

good, hard cry. Why did she feel like she had to hide those feelings from her granddad? From them?

Caleb plopped down next to her on the hay. "You doin' okay, angel May?"

Caleb had a hundred funny little terms of endearment for Harley, and they never failed to put a smile on her face. Except this time.

She nodded slowly, and then changed her mind, shaking it instead. "No. I'm tired. And heavy. I can't seem to find the energy to do anything."

Tyson knelt in front of her. "That's normal, Harley. You just spent the last few weeks in constant motion—staying at the hospital around the clock, and then dealing with the funeral and a never-ending stream of visitors. It's no wonder you're worn out."

"I liked having something to do. When I was busy I could forget—" Her voice broke and Tyson's heart ached.

"We're right here, baby," Caleb said, placing his arm around her shoulders. "Me and Tyson are going to help you get through this."

She didn't respond. Instead her head bowed and her gaze fell to the floor. Tyson wondered if she was trying to hide her tears.

"I can't believe he's gone."

Harley had devoted her entire life to her kid brother. They'd been close as kids, and then, after Johnnie's accident, it was as if Harley's sole focus had narrowed down to a single pinpoint. Her brother.

Playing in the band had been her only escape. And even then, Johnnie served as their "manager," a title Tyson had bestowed on him whenever her brother wheeled into the garage to listen to them practice and give his opinion on their sound and playlist.

She'd been just fourteen—Johnnie eleven—when he'd been thrown from his father's motorcycle. Neither he nor his dad had grabbed helmets as they'd hopped on the bike to check on some cattle in one of the fields. Johnnie had been riding on the back, clinging to his dad, when they hit a deep rut. Johnnie had flown off and hit a rock at a very bad angle. It had left him paralyzed from the neck down.

In a single second, Harley's entire family life had been tossed upside down.

Her dad, John, consumed with guilt, had turned to alcohol. Her mother, Polly, unable to deal with her son's injury, had shut down. Harley had become mother, while Polly became a ghost in her own house. When things got too bad between her parents, they divorced, Polly had remarried within months and moved away from the farmhouse. Her granddad had taken over the rearing of his grandkids, but he owned and operated a large farm, so time wasn't something he had a lot of. Which left far too much responsibility on Harley's young shoulders when it came to caring for Johnnie.

Not that she'd ever complained. It hadn't occurred to her to feel pressure or stress. She stopped talking about college, about growing up and moving out. From that day on, all the pieces of Harley's life appeared to fall into what she considered the proper place, and she didn't question "what if" or "why me".

"I know it's hard to believe now," Tyson said, squeezing her hand, "but this will get easier. It's just going to take some time."

"My dad is in the drunk tank."

The comment had come out of left field.

Or maybe not.

She looked up at Tyson. "Evan called a couple of hours ago. Said he'd gotten a call that my dad was sleeping in someone's yard. When he got there, Dad was passed out cold, reeking of whiskey."

"Everyone handles their grief in different ways." It was a terrible answer. Her dad had been drunk pretty much every night since Johnnie's accident, if you didn't count the rare occasions he decided to dry out for a week or month.

She nodded. "My mom is already back with Art."

Tyson sighed, while Caleb growled. "What about the apartment?"

Harley's mother had decided five minutes before her son's death that she wanted to leave her second husband. An action most people in town supported even though the timing sucked. Art Johnson was a judgmental, holier-than-thou prick.

She shrugged. "Bugsy said he'd let her out of the lease. I think he sort of knew it wasn't going to stick, but he and Granddad are friends and he was trying to help, considering Johnnie…"

Harley didn't seem able to bring herself to actually say the words. To admit that Johnnie was dead. Tyson suspected it would take time for her to come to grips with that fact.

"It was wrong of your mom to throw all that on you while you were dealing with Johnnie's illness and the funeral." Caleb didn't bother to mask the disdain in his tone. Neither of them was fond of Harley's mother. How such a weak-willed, whiny woman had managed to produce two amazing powerhouse kids was completely beyond Tyson.

Harley lifted one shoulder. "Even as we were packing her clothes and loading the furniture on the truck, I knew it was a total waste of time. Anyone need a secondhand bed? Only been slept in twice."

In the past, she'd made light of her parents' problems, but there was no denying this time, she couldn't laugh it off.

Tyson reached for her, merely planning to hug her. At least, that was his original intent. But something happened. He moved forward and Harley lifted her face. Their lips touched and then...

Her arms wrapped tightly around his neck as he cupped her cheeks.

Tyson had indulged in platonic kisses, as well as others that were friendly or lukewarm or the occasional sloppy first attempts back in high school. He'd even experienced some burn-the-house-down kisses with a couple girlfriends at college.

This one blew everything he'd ever known and felt about kissing out of the water. Harley's touch was so ravenous, so passionate, so scorching hot, he was surprised the hay didn't catch fire.

And through it all, he was completely aware, almost hyper in-tune to the fact Caleb was watching the whole thing.

Tyson's hands drifted from her face to her breasts, cupping them firmly, then squeezing. Harley moaned quietly against his mouth. He wasn't sure who pulled back first, but when their lips parted, that's when things really heated up.

Because as Tyson leaned back on his haunches, trying to catch his breath, trying to process what had just happened, Caleb was right there, ready to take his place.

· · ·

TYSON GLANCED up when he heard the sliding door open. Caleb stepped out onto the deck with a cup of coffee in hand. He was dressed for the day, even though it was early.

Tyson was as aware of Caleb's work schedule as he was his own. On Mondays, Caleb's parents opened the Feed and Seed, which Cal took advantage of, sleeping in an extra hour or two. Unlike Tyson, Caleb could sleep until noon without even rolling over. Not that he'd had many opportunities to sleep in lately. Caleb's dad had suffered a minor heart attack a few months earlier and his recovery had been slow. As such, Caleb had taken over the majority of the work, keeping the family businesses running.

Caleb nodded, moving sluggishly to the chair next to his. His friend was a slow mover until he had the first cup or two of strong black coffee in him. "I gotta be back in town at nine for a delivery. Mom was worried Dad would try to overdo it, unloading the truck."

It was unusual for Caleb to join Tyson for what he dubbed his friend's morning meditation. As such, Tyson waited. Caleb was out here for a reason, probably the same reason that had Tyson feeling so uptight and anxious.

"What's on your mind, Cal?"

"Harley looked good last night."

"Yeah, she did," Tyson agreed.

Harley always looked good. Always. And not because she was some fashion plate or glamour queen. In truth, it was rare to see her in anything other than faded jeans and T-shirts. She never curled or styled her dark brown hair. Instead, she just let it hang loose and wavy over her shoulders.

Of course, Tyson hadn't really noticed her beauty until last year. They'd been best friends since God was a baby. Which meant her looks had always taken a backseat to her personality and her talent. Once you've rolled around in a person's head a bit, their hair and clothes don't matter all that much.

His eyes had been opened after one stupid, thoughtless, incredible act, and now he couldn't close them again.

Caleb sighed. "We should have talked to her about those kisses. Not like the three of us to avoid stuff. Used to be we had a problem, we talked it out."

Tyson respected his friend's forthright way of dealing with stuff. There wasn't much that ever hovered in the air between Caleb and his friends. If something was bothering him, Caleb just said it right out and they dealt with it.

Or at least, they had.

Caleb had gone uncharacteristically quiet about the situation. Last year and last night. Tyson should have known that silence wouldn't last.

"The kisses were a problem?" Tyson asked.

Caleb didn't respond to that immediately, but his silence told Tyson the truth more than his words. Caleb didn't regret the kisses anymore than he did.

"You know what I mean." It was a vague answer, but Caleb was right. He understood.

Tyson took a sip of coffee and tried to sort out his thoughts. "She just got back into town, Cal."

"I know. And I didn't sleep a wink last night. How about you?"

"I've had better nights."

Caleb ran his hand through his hair. "You think we were part of the reason why she ran?"

Tyson did, but he also knew they weren't the only thing, or even the main thing, that propelled her out of town as fast as her beat-up Toyota could carry her. "Yeah. I'm sure we were part of it. But there was a lot of shit piling up on her. We can't blame her for wanting to escape for a little while. Losing Johnnie, her folks. Damn, she'd been a powder keg set to go off for years. The time away obviously did her a lot of good. Gave her a chance to figure out who she was without Johnnie. You know what I mean?"

Caleb nodded. "Yeah. She really did look good. Healthy. Happy." Caleb fell silent for just a moment before asking, "You think we're part of the reason she came back?"

Tyson hadn't considered that, but he sure as hell hoped so. "She never intended to stay away forever. Her family is here, the farm, us."

Despite that, Tyson had spent the last year in a state of never-ending anxiety, afraid Harley would decide the grass was greener in Florida.

"She never texted us, never called." It was obvious Caleb had spent a good bit of the last year fretting too. "She's never done that. I didn't like it. Felt like she was avoiding us."

Tyson and Caleb probably should have talked about what had happened at some point in the past twelve months, but— at least from Tyson's perspective—he'd already lost one best friend. He sure as shit didn't want to run the risk of getting into a fight with Caleb over the girl who had left both of them.

"She told us she wasn't going to call. She needed to get away. Completely. We can't be angry at her for that. We supported the decision. Told her she was smart to take a break from all of it."

"She *was* smart to get away from her nutjob parents, but cutting us off—"

"We both kissed her, Cal. At the same damn time. Only a few days after Johnnie's funeral. If that's not adding heat and pressure to a pot that was already boiling over..."

Caleb ran a hand through his hair. "I still don't know why we fucking did that. I've played it over and over in my mind until I've nearly gone crazy."

Tyson didn't reply. He couldn't without revealing that he didn't regret the kiss at all. He loved every second of kissing Harley, and then—shockingly—watching Caleb do the same. It had impacted him in ways he'd never anticipated.

"So we'll clear the air," Caleb added. "Tell her it was a mistake and life can go back to normal."

Tyson knew what Caleb considered "normal", but that standard had changed for him. He'd had too much time to consider what could be.

So he decided to buy himself some time. They'd kissed Harley just one time. Jesus. It wasn't like it was the end of the world or an earth-shattering occurrence. It was a kiss. Well, two actually.

Two long, heated, tongue-tangling, overwhelming kisses that had been cut short and then left on the back burner for way too long.

Perhaps Tyson had built it up in his mind, and maybe he'd spent too much time studying his cousin Jeannette's unusual relationship with her firefighters, Luc and Diego. But kisses like that never ended with just the kiss. They led to more. Like rip off all your clothes and fuck like bunnies for twenty years more.

"Fine. We'll clear the air." Tyson didn't say more, lest he give himself away.

For a moment, things appeared to be settled. Caleb turned

away from him, leaning back in the Adirondack, staring at the lake.

Tyson did the same, though the peaceful scene wasn't making a dent in easing his anxiety.

"She was tense last night," Caleb said after several minutes.

Tyson had noticed that as well. While she'd put on a cheery front, they both knew her well enough to see deeper.

"Yeah. I wondered if it was her dad's presence in the house. She wasn't expecting him to be there. Figure it kind of marred her homecoming."

"Maybe."

While Mr. Mills had eaten dinner at the table, he'd been quiet during the meal and had excused himself afterwards, spending the rest of the evening in his room.

Clearly Caleb wasn't happy with that answer. "I can't put my finger on it, but something tells me she's looking to make some changes. What if she decides to move to Florida permanently?"

Tyson wouldn't—couldn't—let that happen. The time without her here in Maris had been hell. He was in no hurry to repeat it. "We'll convince her not to."

Caleb seemed to consider that, and then, slowly, he nodded. "Yeah. We will."

Tyson felt a ridiculous sense of relief that at least on that front, they were united. Caleb might not want to explore the relationship angle or expand on those incredible kisses, but at least he agreed that Harley belonged in Maris.

And then, because he couldn't deny the truth to himself, he added "with them" to that opinion.

Caleb took a sip of his coffee. "How come you never brought up that day in the barn?"

Tyson lifted one shoulder in a shrug. "Same reason you didn't bring it up either, I guess. I didn't know how you felt about Harley, and I didn't want to take the chance that you'd cut me off as well."

Caleb snorted as if Tyson had said something really stupid. "I wouldn't do that. We're best friends, Ty. Always have been."

"Are you so sure we can both just walk away from her?"

Caleb sighed. "We have to. She won't choose between us. And fuck if I'd ask her to. Last night, for the first time in a long time, my life felt right. I mean, sure, it's fucked up, but…" Caleb seemed to struggle for the words. "When the three of us are in a room together, everything just feels…easy." He leaned his head back against the chair. "That's a stupid word, but I spend so much of my day living up to other people's expectations of me—my folks, our customers, our employees. That all goes away around you two, and I can just be me."

Tyson understood the sentiment only too well. The Feed and Seed was just one of the profitable businesses the Hott family owned and operated in Maris, which meant Caleb's father—along with Tyson's dad, Judge Sparks—were pillars in the community, larger-than-life men who everyone looked up to. Their dads both served on the city council, were officers of the local Lion's Club, and they attended church every Sunday.

And as they got older and more established in their own careers, Tyson and Caleb had assumed some of those same attributes. The expectation was they would follow in their fathers' footsteps, take leadership positions in Maris and serve as role models for the community.

Dr. Tyson Sparks and businessman Caleb Hott, the crown princes. No pressure there.

Tyson blew out a long breath. "I feel the same way, Cal. Things are good when it's just the three of us."

"So we walk away." Even as Caleb spoke the words, Tyson feared it would be impossible for him to give up a dream he'd held on to, had let develop into full-grown desire. Walking away wasn't in his nature. Problem was, he also had a strong sense of right and wrong and, while he was starting to view their situation in shades of gray, he knew there were a lot of folks in town who would not.

Finally, after several tense moments, Tyson nodded. Maybe if he spoke the words, he'd believe them; maybe he'd find the strength to take that first step away. "Yeah. I guess we do."

Caleb glanced toward the front window when headlights flashed along the living room wall. He and Tyson were kicked back in front of the news, winding down from a long day at work.

Four days had passed since Harley's return to Maris, yet neither of them had managed to snag a few minutes alone with her to talk. Both he and Tyson were spending long hours at work—something they'd let get out of hand when Harley was gone. They had tried to meet up with her for lunch or dinner every single day, but she'd offered up excuse after excuse.

Tyson had brought it up as they ate their dinner on their laps in front of repeats of *The Daily Show*, wondering aloud if she was avoiding them.

Caleb had worried about that as well, and they'd decided that—come hell or high water—the girl was going to sit down for a meal with them tomorrow. The damn kiss conversation was long overdue and the sooner they got everything out in the open, the sooner he could start getting some sleep at night. Tossing and turning was not his style, but that was all he could manage this week.

Tyson lowered the footrest of the recliner and went to answer the knock at the door. "Wonder who that could be at this time of night."

Caleb stood up as well when he heard Harley's voice.

"Of course, you're not bothering us. Why would you even ask that? Cal and I were just talking about you over dinner."

Harley preceded Tyson into the living room, smiling when she spotted him.

"Hey, Caleb," she said walking over to give him a friendly hug.

"What's up, buttercup?" Caleb forced the light-hearted tone and was careful to keep the embrace she offered a quick one. Both things were hard to do. For one thing, simply seeing her face again had his dick going hard, and when she leaned closer he caught a whiff of something sweet—peaches?—that made him want to hold her longer, just so he could smell her hair. Jesus.

He'd told Tyson they had to walk away from her, from whatever this was. It was the only way to preserve the friendships. What he hadn't expressed was how fucking hard that was going to be for him.

"I'm sorry I haven't been able to connect with you guys this week," Harley said as she sat on the couch.

Caleb dropped back down in his recliner, but Tyson claimed the spot on the other end of the couch.

"Sounds like you've been busy," Tyson said. "Everything okay on the farm?"

Harley nodded. "Oh, yeah. Everything's great there. You know Granddad. He runs a tight ship. I never had that many actual chores. Someone needed to be in the house most days with Johnnie, so I'm pretty sure my trip to Florida didn't even cause a ripple in the day-to-day routine."

Caleb didn't like to hear Harley downplaying her role on the farm, or how much her presence there meant. Once again, he was struck by the difference in Harley. She had devoted her life to Johnnie, and, while it gave her no pleasure to admit it, to her parents as well. From the time she was fourteen until just over a year ago, she'd been the glue in her family. Not that they'd all stuck together. It was more like they'd simply stuck to *her*, clung to her for support and guidance and anything else they needed. And Harley had carried them along, never breaking under the weight until Johnnie died. "Your granddad missed you like crazy, Harl."

"Oh, I know that. And I missed him. It's just...I actually haven't been at the farm all that much."

"What have you been doing?" Tyson asked.

Harley didn't answer right away. Instead, she took a deep breath, her gaze traveling from Tyson to Caleb and back again.

"Harley?" Caleb leaned forward, resting his elbows on his knees. If she told them she was planning to move away, he'd—God—he'd...

Well, he wasn't sure what he'd do. Lose his temper and tell her she couldn't leave them again. That would be the first thing. Begging came to mind as well, though he didn't like to admit that.

For a brief second, he considered kidnapping her, tying her to his bed until he convinced her to see reason. He dismissed that thought as soon as it flashed because it had his cock growing even thicker and his damn jeans were already uncomfortable.

Tie her to the bed? Not a chair?

Yeah. This was fucked up.

"What are your plans?" he asked.

"I'm afraid you guys will think I'm crazy."

"As long as it doesn't include leaving Maris, we'll be fine with it." Tyson spoke the words Caleb was thinking.

Harley frowned. "Leaving Maris? What? No. Hell no. This is my home. I don't have any intention of leaving here again."

For the first time since he'd seen Harley at her granddad's house, Caleb was able to get some air all the way to his lungs. He could breathe again.

"I've been driving around with Bugsy, looking at property to rent," she finally said.

"For what?" Caleb asked. Bugsy was his family's property manager, and Caleb was a bit annoyed the man hadn't thought to tell him about Harley. Which was stupid, because Bugsy ran the rental end of things exclusively. He never conferred with Caleb or his dad unless there was an issue. And thanks to Bugsy's efficiency, issues were few and far between.

"For the store I hope to open on Main Street. And for a place to live."

Caleb got stuck on the store part. Tyson, meanwhile, found something way more dangerous to latch onto. "You'll live here," he said.

Caleb's gaze flew to Tyson, the words, "What the fuck is wrong with you?" poised on his lips.

Harley beat him to the punch. She laughed, shook her head and said, "Wow. No way. That's a big hell no."

Her quick dismissal of the idea should have set Caleb's mind at ease. Instead, it annoyed him. "Why not?"

Harley clearly hadn't expected Caleb to agree with Tyson's offer. In fact, he *didn't* agree, but knowing what was smart and not saying the opposite wasn't a skill he possessed. He knew what was right. But apparently his dick was the bigger man right now, and it had decided to do the talking.

Harley crossed her arms and sighed. "Fine. You know what, it's time. Let's do this. We kissed. All three of us. At the same time."

And just like that, Caleb was sorry he'd pushed the issue of her living situation. He wasn't ready to talk about the kiss. He'd never be ready. Discussing it with Tyson had been hard enough because so much of what Caleb said had felt like lies.

"It was a mistake," he said slowly, the words coming out thick and heavy. It *had* been a mistake. But not one he regretted. Not even a little bit.

Tyson looked like he wanted to disagree, but Harley didn't give him a chance.

"I know. I was a mess that day. You have no idea how sorry I am. I hope you guys can forgive me for..." The words faded.

Forgive *her*? What the fuck?

Caleb ran through that afternoon in his mind again, trying to figure out where Harley got the idea it was she who'd done anything wrong...

CALEB SAT on the hay bale, watching his two best friends kiss, and he knew in that moment that everything they'd ever thought was real had been a lie. He wasn't jealous of Tyson, and he wasn't embarrassed to be a witness to something they might prefer to do alone. He wasn't angry with them for potentially changing the status quo, and he wasn't going to get up and walk away to give them privacy.

He wasn't going to do anything smart.

The moment her lips left Tyson's, Caleb turned her toward him and added his own fuel to the flames. For a split second, he wondered what Tyson would do. Would he hit him, pull them apart, yell? Would *he* be the one to walk away?

Those thoughts disappeared in an instant when Harley parted her lips and her tongue touched his. Jesus. He'd never been much of a fan of kissing. In his experience, fucking was way more fun than the stuff that came before. With one kiss, one touch, Harley proved that wrong. Big time.

She tasted like strawberry ice cream, smelled like the fresh morning air in spring, and as his fingers slid over the soft skin of her arms, he was reminded of new, clean cotton sheets pulled right from the dryer. Warm, comforting, soothing.

No matter how much he loved kissing her, Caleb couldn't ignore the sensation of Tyson's gaze on them. His friend was watching them the same way he'd watched Tyson kiss Harley. Was Tyson feeling the same thing? The same arousal?

Caleb had watched them knowing he'd never seen anything hotter in his life. And kissing her only sealed the deal, solidified one piece of knowledge that he would never be able to shake.

That he'd never been anywhere righter in his life.

It was maddening, smoldering, steamy, sexy-as-hell insanity.

He gripped her waist tightly, his fingers drifting beneath her T-shirt, seeking skin. Once he found it, he got greedy. Wanted more. He moved them higher, wanting to feel her breasts the way Tyson just had. He took her nipples between his fingers—only the thin cotton of her bra between—and pinched lightly. In his mind, he already had the three of them naked and rolling around in the hay.

The three of them.

That thought gave him a pause and Harley sensed it.

She broke the kiss. Tyson hadn't noticed her hesitance and there was no denying he would have dragged her back into his arms, gone in for a second round. Hell, apparently both he and Tyson were ready to push her down and take it a hell of a lot further than just kissing, but Harley stood up rapidly and stepped away from them, stumbling slightly in her haste to put some distance between them.

Neither he nor Tyson moved, both afraid of shattering whatever it was that had just happened.

Harley's expression didn't reflect theirs. Hers was one of numb confusion. And that's when Caleb saw the first crack, the first fissure.

As far as timing went, theirs sucked. Her brother had just died, her dad had gone on a weeklong bender wreaking havoc all over town, and her mother had decided—for the hundredth time—to leave Art. That decision had lasted all of five days—just long enough for Harley to move her into a new apartment—before her mom decided she wanted to go back. Something she no doubt expected Harley to make happen for her.

She stared at them for several long, painful moments—and then she laughed. Hysterically. Laughed until she cried. And once she started sobbing, there didn't seem to be an end to her misery.

Caleb stood there dumbstruck, kicking himself for being

such an asshole. Tyson moved first, reaching out to pull her into his arms, but she broke free of his grip, moving farther away.

"I c-can't do this. P-please."

Her tear-filled eyes sent daggers through him. Caleb would have done anything—given anything—to take away her pain.

"I have to go," she said. And then, just like that, she was gone.

HARLEY HAD CALLED each of them the next day, told them she was going to Florida for a little while to stay with her aunt. When he'd asked her how long she would be away, she had told him she didn't know. Then she had asked him not to contact her. Had begged him to give her some time to "get her shit together." And because Caleb had been besieged by guilt, he had agreed. As had Tyson.

Maybe if more time had passed between the kiss and her departure, they would have refused her request. Would have told her they were sorry, would have insisted that pushing away their friendship at a time when she needed it most was wrong. But neither of them had done that. They had responded instead with remorse. Both of them would have given her the world on a platter that day if it would have erased the look of absolute devastation in her eyes.

"What are you apologizing for?" Caleb asked.

Harley seemed shocked that he didn't know, but for God's sake, what the hell was she thinking? How could she interpret any part of that day as her fault? They were the ones who'd shown up intent on comforting her, and all they'd done instead was add to the pressure and grief that was already crushing her.

"That day. The way I kissed both of you. And then the way I reacted after. I was a raving lunatic. I don't know how to explain my behavior. It was sort of like everything in my life kept falling in on me until I imploded. Those kisses—dammit—I shouldn't have…"

"*You* shouldn't have?" Tyson's confused tone proved he was as befuddled as Caleb. "What the hell are you talking about, Harley? *I* kissed *you*."

Her brows furrowed and it was obvious she believed she'd initiated the kiss. Caleb had been there, had witnessed the whole damn thing, and in truth, he didn't have a clue who started it. As far as he was concerned, that part didn't matter. What happened after was what mattered.

That, and what happened right now. They were walking on paper-thin ice.

"I reached out for you, Ty," she tried to explain. "You guys had come there to comfort me and I took advantage of your kindness."

Caleb snorted. "Jesus, Harley. If anyone took advantage of the situation, it was us. You were mourning for your brother and we came at you like a couple dogs in heat."

She shook her head, but he cut her off with the wave of his hand. Rising from the recliner, Caleb walked over to her, perching on the edge of the coffee table and reaching for her hands. "Can we just say we were all in a bad place and we did something out of character, unexpected? Let's accept that we're all sorry and move on."

She smiled, the look so sweet, so Harley, that Caleb was

hard-pressed not to use the grip he had on her hand to pull her into his lap and give her something else unexpected.

"I'd like that," she said. "I was so worried you guys would," she shrugged, "I don't know, be so afraid of me and my particular brand of crazy that you'd stay away. I can't tell you what it meant to me when you showed up at Granddad's house the other night. By the way, you got there about five minutes after me," she joked.

"It's Maris, darlin'," Caleb said. "The second you crossed the town line, the birds chirped out in Morse code to let us all know."

She laughed. "It wouldn't surprise me a bit if they did, but I think we all know Eugene called his mother to say I stopped in for gas."

Tyson remained quiet as Caleb and Harley argued over who the bigger gossip was, Eugene's mother or Tyson's Uncle TJ. When his silence lingered too long, Caleb looked over, suddenly concerned Tyson wasn't as willing to put the past away as he'd expected.

"Ty?" Harley prompted.

Tyson's expression was strangely impassive, as if his friend was working overtime to shield his feelings. Typically, the man was an open book, compassionate, funny, honest. Caleb could read everything in Tyson's eyes. Seeing nothing on Tyson's face was slightly unnerving. "If everything is cool between us, there's no reason you can't move in here."

And just like that, Caleb realized that *nothing* was settled between them. They could understand the circumstances, apologize and forgive each other for their actions, but they couldn't wipe away the end result.

Caleb wanted to kiss Harley again. He wanted to do a hell

of a lot more than kiss her. And he didn't doubt for a second Tyson wanted the same.

Glancing at Harley, Caleb felt a sharp stab in his gut as he saw the same desire in her face.

Fuck. This whole situation would be easier if she didn't want them. If she wanted to keep them in the friend zone. Knowing Harley shared the same hunger, the same lust…

Caleb swallowed heavily, fighting to ignore the throbbing in his pants and how hard he had to tense his muscles to keep from moving toward her.

"Tyson," Harley began, clearly ready to launch into her arguments against that idea.

Tyson didn't give her a chance. "It's a huge house, Harl. Four bedrooms, three and a half baths. It was too big for me when I bought it, which is why I invited Caleb to live here."

Tyson bought the house three months after setting up his practice in Maris following his graduation from med school. Caleb had told him he was a fool to keep piling on the debt— the guy had already been swimming in college loans—but Tyson said he was ready to start the next chapter in his life. And that chapter didn't include him living with his parents.

Caleb couldn't fault that reasoning, especially not when Tyson said he could actually help him conquer some of the debt by renting a room until one of them found a wife and started yet another chapter. The house really was too much for one person. Or even two.

But three…

Three might be the perfect fit.

Jesus. What was he thinking? He was as against this as Harley. Or…at least he should be.

"Come here. I'll show you." Tyson took her hand and

tugged her from the couch. They walked down the hall together, still hand in hand, as Caleb followed them. Tyson stopped just outside a closed door, and it was obvious this was the room his friend hoped Harley would move into. The one directly across the hall from Tyson's room and next door to his. If his friend had any sense of self-preservation, he would have offered her the sizable loft upstairs, the one that put some distance between them and the object of their temptation.

Up until that moment, Caleb had always considered Tyson the smart one in their group.

So much for that theory.

Tyson opened the door, revealing a treadmill, some weight equipment and a few boxes of Christmas decorations they'd been too lazy to lug back to the garage.

It was clearly an extra bedroom they'd made the junk room. But it was a nice size and it had its own connecting bathroom, one that was rarely used.

"You can have this room."

Harley looked around at the space to humor them, but she wasn't about to give up the fight. "What about all this stuff?"

Tyson was more than prepared to lob back every volley. "There's room in the garage for all of it."

"But this is your work-out room," she said.

"Me and Cal have been talking about converting the loft into a real workout space. We're going to move the treadmill and weights up there. Add a stationary bike or rowing machine, hook up a TV. Stuff like that."

They'd never discussed doing that. Not once. But Caleb didn't correct Tyson.

"The truth is, I was looking at the smaller, cheaper places

on the west side of town. Until I get my new business off the ground, I don't have a lot of money for rent."

Tyson tilted his head and let her know in no uncertain terms with his bored expression that was her weakest argument yet. "Rent is completely negotiable. Pay what you can afford. Or pay nothing at all."

"Tyson, I wouldn't do that."

Tyson reclaimed her hand. "Why do you want to move away from the farm?"

"I miss Johnnie. It was easier to put that feeling away in Florida because he'd never been there. At the farm, it's like I see him in every room, I hear his wheelchair around every corner. It's my home. It always will be, but I need to create something new, something different, for myself."

"Like the new business?" Caleb asked. She had mentioned it twice now, but Tyson had a one-track mind, only concerned about changing her living situation.

"I want to open a music shop, give guitar and banjo lessons. I talked to Aunt Ginny about it. And Granddad. They both said they would go in as investors, help me set it up. I saved every dime I made working for my aunt in Florida, but it's not enough. I told them I'd prefer to think of their investments as a loan, something I'd pay back. They agreed, but..." She smiled.

"They only said yes to that so you'd go ahead with the plan. Neither one of them will take their money back."

She nodded. "That's what I'm worried about. That, and what if the store fails before I can pay them back. It's one thing to lose your own money, but to lose theirs... I couldn't live with myself. Granddad tried to convince me the money was already mine, my inheritance and," she swallowed heavily, "and the money I would have already earned if I'd gone to college and started a career."

Harley had sacrificed all of that to stay home to care for Johnnie. Gave up on pursuing job offers and earning her own money in order to help her family. Caleb knew her granddad, knew he was aware of everything she'd done, and appreciated that he now had a way to pay her back.

"I want to invest in the store too," Caleb said, wanting to ensure Harley had a real shot at achieving her dreams.

"Wait. What? No. That's not what I was asking."

"I know that," Caleb said, "but Maris needs what you're planning. It's pretty sad that Ty's Collective is all this town has in the way of music. I'll even join you in the venture, so you can add fiddle and mandolin lessons to the list of classes you offer."

"I like that," Tyson said. "Count me in too. I don't have a whole lot of spare time for lessons, but I'd love to contribute some funds."

Harley was shaking her head. "Did you hear what I just said? The store could fail. I'm not looking to take everyone I love down with me."

Tyson crossed his arms. "It's not going to fail. I can already give you a list of names of people who've approached me over the past couple of years to ask for guitar lessons. Most of them are driving all the way to Douglas for their instruments and instruction. This is a great idea, Harley."

She stopped refusing when she heard about the potential interest. "Really? You think folks would come to me for lessons instead?"

"You're part of Ty's Collective. Let's face it, we're Maris musical legends," Tyson joked.

"In *his* mind," Caleb added, chuckling. "There are plenty of people in town looking for what you'd be offering. Trust me."

Their reassurances must have convinced her to move on with her plans. "Cool. Like I said, I've spent a couple of days looking at property, but there was a part of me that was still hesitant to sign anything or move forward. Now," she bit her lower lip before her smile grew, "dammit, I think I'm going for it."

"Bugsy show you anything good?" Caleb asked.

She nodded. "Yeah. There's one place that might work. It's a little bit off the beaten path, but—"

Caleb cut her off. "No. Don't sign anything yet. There's a place two doors down from Logan's shop that's going to be open in less than a month. Jill Prescott is moving her beauty shop to a larger place on Hiatt Street."

Logan owned his own woodworking shop. He sold his creations in the front room while building some of the most amazing furniture in the back. Caleb and Tyson had purchased several of his pieces when they'd moved in here, including the cherry dining room set and the oak coffee table he'd just been sitting on.

Harley's eyes widened. "Jill's shop is moving? She has one of the best locations on Main."

Caleb appreciated her excitement. Jill's place was perfect for what Harley had in mind. Nestled between several other prosperous businesses and in the heart of the town, she'd be in a great position to lure in locals and tourists alike. "Yeah, but her clientele is well established and growing. She didn't have room for another chair in addition to the three she had, so we found her a larger place to rent."

Harley grinned. "One of these days we're going to pull out

a map of Maris, and I want you two to highlight all the places your families own."

Tyson chuckled. "The Sparks' family only owns the restaurant, the hardware store and the bakery. Cal's family is hogging all the rest."

"Just hold off putting your name on any other place. I'll call Bugsy in the morning and let him know we want the store on Main."

"We?" she asked.

"Only condition that comes with landing that store is you let me invest."

Harley rolled her eyes. "Is this you playing hardball?"

It probably meant he had the mentality of a teenage boy, but hearing Harley say the words "hard" and "ball" sent his mind straight to the gutter. "I just think the music store is a great idea. I really want to be a part of it."

She smiled. "Okay. I'd like that. It adds all sorts of pressure for me to succeed, but I can handle it, I guess."

"So it's settled," Tyson said. "You're moving in here and opening your own business."

Harley flashed Caleb an exasperated grin before honing back in on Tyson. "Did you really think you could slip that by me so easily?"

Tyson shrugged. "Hoped I could. Still haven't heard any good reason why you shouldn't move in here."

Those kisses. And what hadn't happened after.

Once the idea of what they'd missed popped into Caleb's mind, it took root. Something told him his friends thought of the same reason as well. The kiss was a precursor and if the timing hadn't sucked, if Harley hadn't cut and run…

Well, Caleb couldn't help but wonder what would have come next.

But none of them said it aloud. Harley and Tyson simply held each other's gazes like middle schoolers in a stare-down…and then she sighed.

"Fine. But I want a lease, and I'm definitely paying rent. How do you guys deal with groceries and stuff?"

"We have a food fund."

She nodded. "Then I'll chip in on that, and utilities and stuff too."

Outwardly, Caleb had watched the entire roommate conversation like a disinterested third party. Tyson hadn't asked his opinion about her moving in and he hadn't offered it. They'd been friends long enough that he could have come right out and said no at any point and they would have listened to his arguments, would have respected his feelings. But he'd pled the fifth, letting his silence be interpreted as his tacit agreement.

Because he *did* want her to move in.

Even though he knew it was a big fucking mistake.

Tyson walked over and peeked into one of the boxes to see what was inside. "We can have this room cleared out by tomorrow night."

Harley laughed. "You don't have to move that fast. I need to figure out furniture and stuff."

"How long will that take?" Caleb asked.

"I don't know. Not long."

"This weekend," Caleb said. "We'll move you in this weekend."

Now that the decision had been made, he didn't want to

wait. Maybe he'd sleep better with her under the same roof. He had to hold back the snort that thought inspired.

Jesus.

He had just basically insured he'd never sleep again.

And for some insane reason, that thought didn't bother him at all.

CHAPTER FIVE

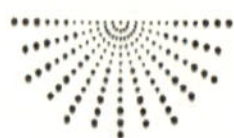

*H*arley looked out across the packed barn and laughed. "I think we've managed to fit every single person in Maris into this place."

Tyson was tuning his guitar, getting ready to play their second set. He followed the direction of her gaze. "Yeah. Think we have."

Not quite two weeks had passed since her return and her life had been a whirlwind since then. Several of the pieces of her previous life had fallen right back into place. She and her father were still giving each other a wide berth, and she had fielded no less than a dozen phone calls from her mother, who once again longed to leave Art, the asshole. The more things changed, the more they stayed the same. At least, as far as her parents were concerned.

As for the band, she, Tyson, Caleb and Logan had gotten together several times to practice, and that was one piece she was glad to see return. When she looked back at her life, the times she was the happiest were when she was on stage with them, making music, escaping in the lyrics, finding their harmonies, creating something special.

With Ty's Collective, she could just get lost for a little while. The world drifted away and nothing mattered except the music. There was no denying it was the guys in the band who had kept her sane all these years…even though lately, two of them were driving her crazy in a good, horrible, constantly horny way.

Despite Tyson and Caleb's best efforts, moving her in with them didn't happen as quickly as they'd hoped. In fact, they'd only just managed to move the majority of her stuff this morning. Tonight would be her first night in her new place, as their roommate.

As far as life decisions went, that was probably her dumbest. And it annoyed her to recall the token resistance she'd put up. She should have just said no flat out. No question, no debate, just no thanks.

Instead, she'd given them a couple lame-ass excuses and then crumbled like a house of cards.

How the hell was she supposed to live with Tyson and Caleb as just friends, just roommates? While she'd left town to mourn Johnnie, another big part of her had used that time to try to get over her infatuation, her sudden obsession, her complete attraction, her deep feelings. Jesus, she didn't have enough names for what she felt.

For her *two* best friends.

So much for that. She'd been back in Maris less than an hour before they'd arrived at the farm. She'd run straight into their arms, and any hope she'd had that those kisses were a fluke or something she had built up in her mind faded. Now all she could think about was kissing them again.

And again.

And then doing a lot more than kissing.

It would have been easier to dismiss the idea of sleeping with both of them as complete insanity if she hadn't run into Jeannette, Diego and Luc at Sparks Barbeque three days ago.

She'd popped in to pick up some lunch, looking forward to getting back into the local social scene. She had missed so many people in Maris, and it was pretty much guaranteed most of them would be at the restaurant. Mainly because a lot of them worked there. Harley had grown up with Tyson's cousins, and she called them friends. While she had enjoyed the time in Florida, she had longed for some female companionship—with women her own age.

Macie had been behind the bar. Two seconds after she'd walked into the place, she had found herself wrapped up in a huge embrace by the vivacious bartender. And then Adele. And then Tyson's kid sister, Paige, and finally Jeannette, who'd come out of the kitchen when she'd heard all the loud squeals and laughter.

Luc and Diego, Maris' two hunky firefighters, were sitting at the counter. Jeannette, who had always been so shy and quiet, walked over to them, planting a sultry kiss on Luc and then an equally hot one on Diego.

Macie had laughed at Harley's shell-shocked expression, and then explained the threesome were an item.

Threesome.

Everything had changed in that moment. The hopes and desires Harley had been slightly ashamed of, that she had dismissed as impossible, suddenly didn't seem so unreasonable.

Which was a ridiculous thought.

Because it was still impossible.

Luc and Diego had always been…well…a couple. It hadn't been unheard of for them to take women out together on dates, even before Harley left town. But the locals chalked it up to the two men being from "the city," and then they dismissed it as youthful fun.

They'd never, ever seriously dated anyone, and certainly not anyone from one of Maris' first families—the Sparks' clan.

Harley looked across the barn and found Luc, Diego and Jeannette sitting at a table, all three of their heads close together as they talked. Luc was holding her hand, while Diego had his arm wrapped around her shoulder. Every now and then, one of the men would sneak a kiss.

"You get used to it."

Harley jumped slightly, startled to discover Tyson next to her. He could tell what she was looking at.

"You're used to it? I mean, she's your cousin. It doesn't bother you that they…?" Harley wouldn't finish that thought aloud if someone held a gun to her head. Talk about awkward.

Tyson grinned. "No. I'm not going to pretend it didn't catch me off guard at first. Mainly because Jeannette was always so quiet and, well…a lot's happened since you left town. Luc and Diego are perfect for her. Only a fool would begrudge them what they have. It's special. And it works."

Only a fool.

Harley let those words rattle around in her mind as Tyson walked over to Caleb, the two of them leaning closer as they made sure they both found the right key on their instruments.

Logan was standing at the edge of the stage, talking to Lacy. Harley was delighted the two of them had found each other. There was no denying they were a perfect couple.

When she'd been in Florida, a year had felt like a lifetime *and* the blink of an eye. Now that she was back, she realized that was true for Maris as well.

Time hadn't stood still here as much as she'd always thought when she was growing up. In her youth, she swore that nothing ever changed in Maris. Her time away proved that wrong.

She was standing in a room full of family and friends, people she had known her entire life, and it felt like she didn't know a damn thing about them anymore.

"Should we start the next set?" Tyson asked.

She nodded slowly, still distracted as she glanced around the barn.

"Everything okay, Harl?" Caleb had noticed she was preoccupied.

"Yeah. Just thinking it's going to take me a while to figure out what's changed and what's the same around here. Even before I left last year, I was sort of out of things for a few months. Johnnie was sick for a while. I think I forgot to look around."

Caleb reached out to take her hand, squeezing it comfortingly. "We'll help you catch up."

That was another thing that had changed. The way Tyson and Caleb touched her. The tomboy in the group, she was used to roughhousing from them. They'd ruffle her hair; she'd punch them on the arm. They'd playfully pat her ass; she'd whack them on the back of the head. It was fun, harmless. The way things used to be.

Now they were gentler. They held her hand and wrapped their arms around her shoulders just like Luc and Diego were doing with Jeannette. Apparently this was the new normal.

And it wasn't helping her get over her feelings. It was making them worse.

Fortunately, Ty took his place behind the microphone. She walked next to him—her usual spot on his left. Caleb stood on the right, with Logan next to him on the end. People began to yell out requests and for the next two hours, she struggled to find that peaceful place.

Sadly, it had disappeared. She was too in tune with other things to get lost in the music this time.

There were too many things to see. The way Luc spun Jeannette on the dance floor, straight into Diego's waiting arms, the three of them laughing, despite the disapproving glances from Eugene's mom, Phyllis, and her sewing circle friends. There was no mistaking the judgmental glances and sideways comments.

Then she caught sight of her dad, standing near the door. She had expected—hoped—he would stay away tonight. The barn parties were BYOB and very few people came without coolers of their drink of choice. He caught her looking at him and gave her a hesitant smile before she glanced away.

Even her mom was in attendance tonight, which was a big surprise. And no surprise at all. The second she found out Harley was back, her mother was on the phone, begging her to help her leave Art, swearing that this time it would stick.

Art Johnson, Mom's second husband, was a Grade A douchebag. While he'd never physically abused her mom, it was safe to say he'd done a number on her head. Harley had been trying, unsuccessfully, for twelve years to get her mom away from the guy. Sadly, Mom always made excuses for her husband's temper or his jealousy or his holier-than-thou approach to basically everything and everyone. Despite

Mom's constant backpedaling, Harley kept trying to get her mom away, kept hoping that one time the separation would stick, because the guy was a total bastard.

Of course, Art had no love for Harley either. Art took "devout Christian" to new levels, criticizing Harley's clothing if he considered it too revealing or lecturing her on how she shouldn't be performing on stage, and his favorite nickname for her was sinner, followed closely by whore. Yeah, the guy was a real winner.

He gave Harley a hard time every time she absconded with Mom, blaming her for ruining his marriage.

Art would find out her mom was here tonight—he always did—and he would give her holy hell for it. Tell her she was wrong to listen to their music—the devil's music. Art believed the only singing anyone should ever do was in church, and it should only be hymns.

Which meant Harley could count on a long, crying phone call from her mother tomorrow.

And then there was one thing she *wasn't* seeing.

The main thing.

Johnnie wasn't there, sitting in his chair right in front of the stage. Her biggest fan, he called himself. It was her granddad who had started hosting the barn parties, so that Johnnie could watch them perform. He'd always claim a spot front and center, only leaving it when Macie dragged him and his wheelchair out to the floor for a dance.

In the midst of that memory, she realized they were playing Johnnie's song. God, they were already halfway through the thing and she hadn't remembered. Harley messed up a chord and Tyson glanced over, giving her an encouraging wink, a reassuring smile.

Shit. She needed to stop looking around, stop thinking.

Just stop.

Yeah. Her mind was whirling a mile a minute. Nothing was going to stop this merry-go-round, until she got so dizzy she fell off.

It was a fast-paced song and she was struggling to keep up.

She needed to concentrate on what was happening on the stage because it was her turn to showcase her playing. Looking down, she let her fingers pluck out the melody, the motions almost second nature to her. For a brief time, the music did the trick. She focused solely on the strings, the notes. It centered her. Helped her find her way back.

At last, the song ended and a new one began. And then another. She forced herself to push away her memories of Johnnie.

It was easier now that the song her brother had always loved was over and the spotlight was off her. During this number, the focus moved to Caleb, who ran the bow along the fiddle at the speed of light. Typically, she loved hearing the music that flowed from his instrument, but all Harley noticed tonight was the strong muscles in his arms as he moved, the way his jeans fit him just right as he tapped his toe in time with the beat, and the slow slide of just one bead of sweat as it rolled along his cheek, getting caught in the five o'clock shadow that was sexy as shit.

Her pussy clenched.

Whoa. Where did that come from?

Harley blew out a breath and averted her eyes. Looking at Caleb was not helping. It was just screwing with her head in a much different way.

Then Tyson took the lead again, strumming his guitar

with such skill, Harley couldn't help but watch, wondering what it would feel like if he put those fingers to use on her in the bedroom. She could still recall the way he'd gently cupped her cheeks in the barn that day. The way he'd used that soft grip to hold her in place as he kissed her.

There was nothing hotter than a man who could sing, and Tyson's voice tonight was sending sparks along her spine, jolts of electricity to every erotic zone in her body.

She licked her lips when he glanced her way, her gaze locked on his mouth, watching it move, imagining…

She missed her cue. They were on the chorus and she was supposed to sing backup. Tyson was looking at her curiously.

Harley joined in on the next line and Tyson smiled, turning his head away once more.

So basically, she couldn't look anywhere. Not at her family or the crowd and definitely not at the band. She couldn't very well stand here the rest of the night with her eyes closed.

She found a spot on the back wall of the barn where her granddad had hung up his "lucky" horseshoe. It was just low enough to fool people into thinking she was looking at them. For the next three songs, she never took her eyes off it as she concentrated on her playing.

She still wasn't able to fall into that sweet contentment she longed for. It was taking too much of her energy simply to focus on the chords and the lyrics instead of Tyson's lips and Caleb's firm ass and Jeannette swirling around in Harley's dream life, Phyllis Barton's scowl.

And Johnnie.

She'd never felt his absence more intensely than at this moment. He would know what to say to make all the shit swirling around in her head go away. He'd been her sounding board, her conscience, her counselor, her…everything.

When they finally finished playing the second encore, Tyson called a halt to their concert, reminded everyone to drive safe, and she was free at last to make her getaway.

She unplugged her banjo and put it in the case quickly, ignoring the people who'd come up to the stage to thank them for a great night. She let Tyson, Caleb and Logan handle the brief interactions that always followed the show.

Harley needed air. Lots of fresh air.

Escaping out the back door, she was able to avoid the crowd of folks taking their leave in the front of the barn. Car doors opened and closed, people called out goodbyes and engines started. A steady stream of taillights pierced the darkness of the night as everyone left.

Harley kept walking away from the barn until the voices faded. She was halfway to the second barn, the one that actually served some farming function, when she heard her name being called.

She ignored it and walked faster.

"Harley."

It was Tyson. Though she'd really hoped to find somewhere quiet to get her shit together, she knew he would only follow her if she didn't answer.

Turning, she was completely unsurprised to find Caleb with him. They were cutting the distance between them and her quickly.

"You okay?" Tyson asked.

"Yeah," she lied. "It was really hot in there. I thought I'd take a breather, try to cool off."

Neither man bought it.

"You want to revise that answer?" Caleb asked in that gruff manner he had. God help the man's future children because they'd never get away with a damn thing.

"He wasn't there."

She didn't have to say more than that. They knew who.

Harley swiped at her nose, which was suddenly running, while blinking rapidly to try to dry up the tears she really didn't want to fall.

Both actions were pointless when Tyson stepped closer and pulled her into his arms.

"I missed him too," he murmured.

So much for not crying. She wrapped her arms around his waist, clinging to him, hiding her face in his chest as the tears rolled down her cheeks.

Caleb stepped closer, behind her, his large, strong hand stroking her back slowly.

Neither of them said anything as she quietly fell apart. And then, eventually, she pulled herself back together.

When she felt ready to face them again, she released Tyson and took a step back. He thrust a hankie in her hand and she laughed.

"Oh my God. Are you still carrying these? What are you? Ninety?" She and Caleb had teased Tyson for years about the extremely old-fashioned handkerchiefs he constantly tucked in his back pocket.

The original ones he carried had been a treasured gift from his grandfather. It was Grandpa Tom who had taught Tyson that a prepared man always had a hankie. Harley had thought Tyson carried them as a tribute to the beloved man after his death, but as more years passed and he bought new ones to replace the old, she realized he just really liked having a handkerchief at the ready.

"Need me to show you how to use it?" Tyson lifted the soft, well-worn cotton from her hand to her face, wiping away the tears. "Joke all you want, but you'd be a mess right now if I weren't here to save the day."

It was hard to argue with that logic because she didn't have a tissue and, well, she *was* a mess.

"Thanks," she said. "Sorry about that. Every time I think I get my grief under control, something sneaks in and blind-sides me."

"We should have realized tonight would be rough," Caleb said. "Stupid of us to go in there without..."

Without what?

Like Caleb, she couldn't think of one thing they could have done to make the night easier. Short of what they'd done. Played through it.

"It's okay, Cal," she said. "We did what we had to do. Hopefully, as more time goes by, it'll hurt less."

Caleb shook his head, obviously feeling some sort of guilt. "I shouldn't have started the 'Orange Blossom Special.'"

It was the song she'd lost her way on, the one that had distracted her. Johnnie's favorite. Typically when they played it, Macie would take Johnnie out of the floor, put him in the center of the circle and everyone would dance to the frantic, frenetic, fast-paced song as Johnnie laughed.

Macie hadn't moved tonight. No one had. Harley hadn't even realized it until that moment. They'd played the whole song, but not one person had danced.

And that thought made her even sadder.

She looked at Tyson. "Tell Macie to start the dance next time."

Tyson nodded. "Okay. I will. Listen, Harley. I know the plan was for you to spend tonight at our place, but if you feel like you want to stay on the farm—"

"No. I don't want to stay here. I have a new home now. Kind of looking forward to trying this roommate gig with you guys."

Caleb chuckled, wrapping his arm around her shoulder as the three of them headed back to the party to break down the stage and grab their instruments. "We probably should have warned you, we're not exactly the neatest guys."

Tyson added to the list. "And the fridge is usually empty. We've mastered takeout and eating out. Pretty much champs at that."

"And I never remember to finish the laundry. Good at loading the washer and running it, but—"

"But then two days go by before he remembers he started it and by then it stinks and he has to wash it again," Tyson finished.

"There's always gonna be a handful of dishes in the sink too," Caleb added, pointing at Tyson, who grinned sheepishly. "His."

"Yep. They're mostly my coffee cups. I only wash them when I run out of clean ones."

She grinned. "God. Wish you'd told me all this before I moved my stuff. Anything else?"

Caleb nodded. "We watch sports on TV. About ninety percent of the time. Other than that, it's the news and *River Monsters.*"

She feigned a shudder. "Jesus. *River Monsters* might be a deal breaker."

"What?" Tyson asked, his brows lifted. "That is the greatest show ever."

She shook her head. "Not even close. I'm going to have to insist that *Game of Thrones* and *Chopped* be added to the list of acceptable viewing."

"What the hell is *Chopped*?" Caleb asked.

"You'll see," she said as they entered the barn.

"There you are," Granddad said, walking up to them as soon as they reappeared. "I was starting to worry." He zoned in on her face instantly. She figured there was no hiding the puffy, red eyes. "You okay?"

"Yeah." Then she realized he looked stressed. "Are *you*?"

Granddad hesitated, then said, "I can't find your dad. He's not in the house or here."

"Great." Harley wasn't so keen on being thrust back into the nightmare that was her parents. Between her mom's constant phone calls and now this sinking feeling that said her dad had fallen off the wagon again, she wondered why she'd ever left Florida to come back.

"Harley. It'll be okay," Granddad said, distractedly. "I'll find him. I'm an old man and I'm overreacting. Your dad is a grown man and perfectly capable of..."

His words faded. There was too much water under that bridge for either of them to avoid thinking the worst. And there was no way she'd leave her grandfather alone to find, well, whatever it was they were going to find.

"We'll go look for him," Tyson said, his hand resting briefly on her lower back, placed there to bolster her.

"I'll check the other barn. Ty, you can circle the corrals,

and Mr. Mills, you want to look around the backyard and in the other outbuildings?" Caleb asked.

And…just like that, she remembered exactly why she came back to Maris.

She came back for Tyson and Caleb. She loved them. And she feared/realized/was beginning to accept that she was *in* love with them too.

Granddad nodded. "Yeah. That sounds good."

"I'll check the house again," Harley offered. Her dad had better hope she wasn't the one to find him. In her present state of mind, she wasn't sure what she'd do.

"Okay, everybody got their phones?" Caleb asked. When they nodded, he instructed them to text if they found him, and then they all took off in separate directions.

Harley entered the farmhouse, walking straight upstairs to her dad's room. It was empty, just as Granddad had said. So she searched through the rest of the rooms on the second floor before coming back downstairs.

She'd just reached the foot of the stairs when she realized there was a slice of light coming from behind the closed door of Johnnie's room.

Harley approached it slowly. She hadn't been back in Johnnie's room since returning to Maris. Her granddad kept the door closed, and she hadn't asked him what he had done with Johnnie's stuff. Was it all still there or had Granddad cleaned it out? Both answers bothered her, and she had decided she didn't really want to know.

Slowly, she turned the knob, trying to still her racing heart. Her emotions were riding too close to the surface tonight.

Peering around the half-open door, she blinked, trying to figure out if she was seeing what she thought she was seeing.

Her mom and dad were sitting on the side of Johnnie's bed, their backs to her.

Her mom was crying, and Dad was comforting her.

Harley stood there stunned for a full minute before she quietly closed the door, not wanting to intrude on…on what?

What the hell was that? Her parents hadn't spoken to each other in years, beyond a cordial hello when their paths crossed.

Harley walked back out of the house and sank down on the top step of the porch. For twelve months, she'd mourned Johnnie's death alone. The solitude she'd created had given her the false sense that she had been the only one grieving. It was a ridiculous feeling because she knew her grandfather had been devastated as well.

But Harley had been too far away and too wrapped up in her own misery to acknowledge that, so she'd felt completely alone.

Tonight proved that wrong. Proved *her* wrong.

"Harley."

She glanced up when Granddad called her name.

"Dad's inside."

Granddad nodded. "Yeah. I just slipped in through the back door. I saw. Didn't think to check there the first time. Near as I can tell, your dad's never gone in there since Johnnie passed." Granddad didn't seem to be as dumbfounded by the discovery as she was. In fact, he didn't look a bit surprised. Instead, he reached into his pocket. "I have something for you."

Harley blinked a couple of times, certain she couldn't be

seeing what her granddad was holding out to her. "I don't understand."

"I think it's time for you to take this back."

Granddad held a dream catcher she'd made shortly after Johnnie's accident. She had only been a month or so into her ninth grade year when she'd fashioned the silly thing. Her summer break that year had been consumed by fear and worry and numbness as Johnnie fought for his life in the hospital—he'd only been eleven.

How many times had she thought those words that summer?

He's only eleven.

The month at the hospital was followed by the upheaval in the house as everything was rearranged so that her brother's bedroom could be moved downstairs, and so that he could maneuver his wheelchair around the rest of the house easily.

There hadn't been time to go school shopping, so Harley was still using what was left of her school supplies from middle school. She was looking through her tatty book bag one day on the bus home, trying to sort out the trash from what she needed. Amongst the garbage was what she'd decided were the perfect makings for a dream catcher.

As the bus stopped at farm after farm, she twisted some old wire and yarn together in a circle, then wove the string she and her girlfriends used to play Cat's Cradle in a spider's web pattern in the middle. She added some beads to the long tail she created and tied on two bird feathers she'd found on the playground during recess way back in seventh grade. Then, as a lark, she added a cactus charm she'd received as a prize from her teacher when she'd won the class spelling bee.

The moment she stepped off the bus, she ran the entire

way down the long driveway, anxious to give the dream catcher to Johnnie as a gift. She knew he dreamed of escaping the wheelchair, and she wanted the same thing as well.

She wanted her brother back—the one who could play tag, go creek walking, climb trees, ride horses and do all the things they'd always done together. She believed the dream catcher would grant them both their greatest desire. Johnnie had been delighted by the gift and she'd hung it above his bed, as they wondered aloud how long it would take for the magic charm to work.

However, as more time passed, it became obvious he would never walk again. Harley began to resent the dream catcher—the way it built up her childish dreams only to dash them. She had truly believed—and so had Johnnie.

Soon she decided the thing was evil. That it was actually a talisman that captured dreams to hold them hostage and prevent them from coming true. She tried a couple of times to take it down, but Johnnie stopped her. Told her it was a gift from her and he loved it.

She didn't have the heart to take it from him, but it had started to serve as a constant reminder of how she'd let him down. Harley hadn't been able to make his dream come true.

Then that feeling revealed itself more clearly. It was *her* dream that hadn't been realized. The brother who could run and play with her hadn't returned. And that left her feeling guilty.

The day after Johnnie died, she went into his room and ripped the dream catcher off the wall, tossing it into the trashcan in the corner.

Seeing it now in her granddad's hand, she realized he'd found it, taken it out of the garbage.

"Granddad. How—"

"I think you gave up on *your* dreams too soon."

Harley didn't know how to reply. Her dream had been for her brother to walk again. Not only did she not get that dream, but he died. That sure as fuck hadn't been her dream. A wave of anger bubbled up inside her.

Granddad looked toward the front door of the house, no doubt remembering her parents in Johnnie's room. "A lot of people gave up after that accident."

"I didn't give up."

He smiled at her in a way that told her he didn't agree. "Sweetheart. Your ambition in middle school was to go to college, to become a vet. And the summer after fifth grade, you playacted your future wedding in that backyard so many times, making poor Johnnie be the groom, that I had to start giving him money to continue. You drove the boy crazy with that game, but you loved it so much. Loved the idea of a fancy wedding and true love and happily ever after."

She laughed and cried at the memory. Then she said what she'd always felt, always believed. "It didn't feel right for me to go off and have a life when he couldn't."

Granddad shook his head. "Harley, Johnnie was the only one in this family who *did* have a life after that accident. He was the only one unafraid to live, the only one fighting to make every single day count. Think about it, girl."

Harley let her mind drift back over the years, over Johnnie's weekly "lunch date" with Macie at Sparks. The way he "danced" in the middle of that circle in the barn. Harley always thought it was Macie leading the charge to the floor, but now that she thought about it, it was Johnnie who got everyone out there, spinning around and dancing like he didn't have a care in the world.

The way he raced his wheelchair all over the ranch like some sort of daredevil. The way he was never—God, *never*—without a smile or a joke or some sarcastic comment. He was a voracious reader, an incredible poet, and one of the smartest, most *alive* people she'd ever known.

And even when he was in the hospital that last month before he died, he had looked her right in the eye and told her he'd had a good life and that he didn't regret a thing.

She'd pushed those words away, let her anger over his dying so young bury them deep. Maybe he didn't regret stuff, but at the time, she'd had enough resentment for both of them.

"You're right," was all she could say in reply. Granddad was absolutely right. Then, because she was a Mills and that meant she had too much pride to ever admit a wrong without a fight, she added, "But I *am* moving on. I'm renting that room at Ty's house."

Granddad nodded slowly. "That's not moving on, Harley. That's just moving. I want to make sure you understand that it's time to open up your heart. Dig deep. Find some new goals and maybe dust off one or two of the old ones you gave up on. Start living."

He held out the dream catcher. "Start dreaming again."

She hesitated just a moment before reaching out to take the dream catcher.

And crazy as it seemed, the second she held it in her hand, her heart felt lighter. The pressure on her chest lifted.

Johnnie had touched so many people. His life had

mattered. To her, to Granddad, to Tyson and Caleb and Macie.

She wanted her life to matter too.

Aunt Ginny's words drifted back to her, and for the first time, Harley really took them to heart.

Have enough adventures for both of you.

She was ready. Glancing heavenward, she silently sent up a question to her beloved brother. *I can do this, right?*

In her mind, she saw Johnnie smiling at her, offering her a wink that made her feel the way it always did. Like she could take on the world and win. Then she imagined that sardonic tone of his saying, "What took you so long?"

Hastily, she dug her phone out of her back pocket. "Found him," she texted when she recalled that Caleb and Tyson were still frantically searching for her father. "He's fine."

The guys returned and she simply explained that her dad was in Johnnie's room and needed some privacy. Neither of them questioned it.

And twenty minutes later, they'd loaded their instruments in Caleb's SUV, waved goodbye to her granddad, and Harley was headed to her new home. Her new life.

Jeannette's happy face flashed before her, and something else that had been fuzzy and out of focus became crystal clear too.

Caleb drove, while Tyson sat shotgun. She was in the backseat alone as they flew by trees and houses. She didn't see any of it.

Instead, she imagined the future she wanted. It would take some work. Hell, it would probably take a miracle.

But she didn't care. She'd do whatever it took.

Because she was setting off on a new adventure.

CHAPTER SIX

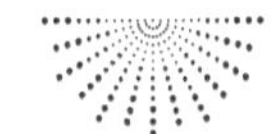

Tyson sat in his usual spot on the deck, coffee in hand, soaking up the stillness of Sunday morning. Harley had been quiet on the way home last night, but he figured that was to be expected. In addition to dealing with her sadness over Johnnie, she'd moved out of her childhood home.

It had been well after midnight when they returned. She had given each of them a hug—and a soft kiss on the cheek—and then said good night.

Tyson had sort of expected his sleep to be restless with Harley so close, but surprisingly, he'd slept deeper than he had since before she'd taken off to Florida. There was something comforting about knowing she was close. It set his mind at ease.

At last.

"Morning."

He glanced over his shoulder to find Harley standing at the French doors.

"Am I interrupting?" she asked.

"Interrupting?"

She grinned. "Caleb said you have some sort of morning meditation routine you follow."

Tyson gestured to the Adirondack next to him. "That's Cal's way of saying I'm a morning person. I just like sitting out here with my coffee. It's peaceful."

She sat down and glanced out across the lake. "Wow. It really is. I've been here before for parties and stuff, but I never really appreciated the view. Seeing it now, with the sun reflecting on the water, the mist hovering just above the surface. It's gorgeous."

He watched her as she spoke and couldn't fault her observations. This morning's view was the most beautiful he'd ever seen. And the lake had nothing to do with it.

"You're right. It is."

Harley flushed slightly when she realized he was looking at her. She was in what he assumed were her pajamas, a faded Texas Rangers T-shirt and colorful boxer shorts. Her wavy, dark brown hair was held up in a ponytail. It had grown several inches since she'd left and he liked it longer. Her skin was naturally tanned and her thick eyelashes framed her deep brown eyes perfectly without mascara or any of that other stuff women used.

He couldn't force himself to stop staring. After so long apart, he felt as if he needed to figure out what had changed and what was the same with her. He'd known her his entire life, but he'd never looked at her with these eyes.

Eyes that desired. That adored. That hungered.

Harley turned to face him straight on. "What? Is there something on my face?"

He blinked when he realized he was probably creeping her out. "No. I just missed you."

She gave him a crooked grin. "I've been back for two weeks, Ty, and we've seen each other almost constantly the past three days. I would think by this point you and Cal would be sick of me already."

The three of them spent one full day rearranging the furniture in his house, making room to incorporate her stuff. Then another day boxing up her clothing, her knick-knacks and whatnot at the farm, before spending most of yesterday morning lugging it all here, setting up her bedroom suite and getting her settled. Then, they'd spent hours onstage together last night. Tyson considered himself to be in good shape, but he couldn't deny more than a few muscles were stiff and sore this morning.

But he wasn't sick of her. Far from it.

"Your hair is longer."

Her eyes narrowed in confusion. God, he was blathering on like an idiot. If he weren't careful, he'd start reciting freaking poetry to her.

She reached up and played with her ponytail. "Yeah. I need to get it cut."

"Don't." Harley's frown deepened when he added, "I like it long."

"Are you okay?"

Tyson chuckled. For the past week, he'd been giving himself a constant pep talk. Something along the lines of *keep your hands to yourself*. Now that she was here, he couldn't even keep his eyes to himself. And he was having a hard time remembering why he had to. "Yeah. I'm good, Harl. Really good."

"Jesus, not you too," Caleb growled at Harley as he joined them on the deck. "What the hell is wrong with sleeping in on a Sunday morning? Y'all are aware it's only eight thirty, right?"

Harley giggled. "I was too excited to sleep."

"Excited about what?" Caleb asked.

She lifted one shoulder casually. "I don't know. Being here, I guess. Everything's been happening so fast since I got home, I haven't had a chance to let it all soak in."

Though she probably wouldn't ever say it aloud to them, Harley hadn't had the opportunity to try many new things. She'd devoted her life to her home, to her brother, giving up college and even a lot of opportunities to date.

She'd had one long-term boyfriend, Juan, when he and Caleb were away at college. Juan, a carpenter, lived and worked in the neighboring town of Douglas. The relationship ended when Juan started talking marriage. Harley hadn't been averse to it, but when she mentioned that she wanted Johnnie to come live with them eventually, Juan backed away. Which, in Ty's opinion, showed the man's true colors. He'd never been a Juan fan, but Harley had insisted while they were dating that he was a nice guy. She'd revised that opinion when Juan had asked Harley to choose between him and her brother.

Tyson was glad she considered this move a good thing, something that made her happy. There was very little he wouldn't do to put a smile on her face, to take away the pain she'd suffered since Johnnie's death.

God knew it made him happy to have her here. And one glance at Caleb's amused expression told him his friend felt the same.

"Give it a couple of weeks," Caleb joked. "The bloom should be off the rose by then."

"So what's the Sunday routine around here?"

Caleb looked at him and Tyson shrugged. "Not sure we have one. Life on the lake is a lot different than one on the farm. We just sort of do whatever."

"No chores?"

Tyson shook his head. "We do stuff whenever we feel like it. Or whenever it needs to be done."

"Wow. That's gonna take some getting used to. We all had daily chores at home. And then there was a schedule for Johnnie's medicine and physical therapy and, even in Florida, my aunt and I had a routine of sorts. We'd have breakfast together, open the store, stock the shelves and stuff like that. After we closed, we'd take a walk on the beach and then make dinner, watch *Jeopardy*." She rolled her eyes when she begrudgingly admitted that part.

"What are you? Ninety?" Tyson teased.

She smirked. "All I'm saying is, it's nice to have some sort of daily plan."

Caleb placed his empty coffee cup on the deck beside his chair. "We do have daily plans. Monday through Friday. They're called 'get up and go to work'. The weekends are when we throw convention out the window and let the spirit move us where it will."

"Fine," she conceded. "So where is the spirit moving you today?"

Tyson laughed. "It doesn't work that way. Just sit back and relax, Harley. We're grownups now. No one is yelling at us to do our chores, and if we want to have beer and ice cream for dinner, we can."

She crinkled her nose. "We're not having beer and ice cream for dinner tonight, are we?"

Caleb snorted. "Maybe. Tell us about the plans for your store."

They sat on the deck for two full hours, each of them taking turns filling the coffee cups. During one of her trips for refills, Harley came back with a heaping plate of toast. Apparently the spirit had told her she was hungry.

It was the first time since she'd returned that things between them had felt like old times. The three of them had never struggled for conversation, and while the elephant was still sitting in the corner, waiting for his turn to stomp on them, it was easy to pretend that all was well with the world again.

"I'm so bummed I missed the bachelorette party," Harley said after Tyson told her about the countdown to his cousin Sydney's wedding to her high school sweetheart, Chas.

"By the way," Tyson said, "I still need a date for the reception. You want to go with me?"

Caleb frowned. "I was going to ask her."

Harley laughed. "How about all three of us just go stag together?"

It was on the tip of Tyson's tongue to tell her to take the word "stag" out and she had a deal, but Caleb answered first—and more wisely.

"Sounds like a plan. It's a month away. And I should warn you, Sydney's asked us to play the song for her first dance with Chas."

"Just the one song?" Harley asked.

Tyson started to take a sip of his coffee, then put it down. He was on cup number four. Time to switch to water. "She didn't hire us to play for the reception because we weren't sure you'd be back, and she said she wanted us to enjoy the party."

Harley stood up and walked to the railing of the porch. "Cool. Maybe we can start practicing the song later. After…"

"After?" Caleb prompted.

"Would your spirits be interested in taking a dip in the lake with mine?"

Tyson grinned. "I think they could be convinced. I'm stiff as hell after yesterday."

Harley's gaze drifted toward his lap. "Stiff, huh?"

Shit. Well, *now* he was.

What the hell was she doing? Throwing around sexy innuendoes and looking at him with those bedroom eyes. If he didn't know better, he'd think she was flirting.

"Harley," he started, but she turned away from him before he could figure out what to say next.

"The water looks nice and cool." Harley started down the steps that led from the deck to the path to the dock.

"Aren't you forgetting something?" Caleb called out.

She looked at him curiously. "I don't think so."

"Your bathing suit."

"Oh," she laughed. "Nope. Didn't forget. My spirit is skinny-dipping."

It took Tyson a full minute to process what she'd said— and then another minute to try to force some of the blood in his body away from his cock and back to his brain.

"Fuck," Caleb muttered.

Tyson owned a fair bit of the property on either side of him and the land directly across the lake was undeveloped. Nothing but the woods. That privacy had ensured more than a few of his parties had ended up with skinny-dippers diving off the dock. Hell, he, Caleb and Harley were usually the ones leading the charge.

This time…

"We can't do this," Caleb said.

Tyson appreciated Caleb's concern. But he didn't agree.

"Actually, my spirit says I can."

Caleb scowled. "That's not your spirit. That's your dick."

"How'd you sleep last night, Cal?"

"What the fuck are you talking about?"

Tyson turned and faced his friend. "How did you sleep?"

Caleb sighed. "Like a fucking baby."

"She's supposed to be here. With us. You want to keep denying that?"

"You're the smart one, Tyson. Start thinking with the right head. Play this whole scenario out to the end and tell me what you see."

Tyson had done that. A million times in the last twelve months. And he'd seen the same thing Caleb had.

The disapproval on their fathers' faces.

The scorn of people in town that they respected.

Their mothers' concern.

Caleb would lose business. Tyson would most likely lose patients.

"Jeannette—" Tyson started.

"That's a different situation and you know it."

Tyson *did* know that, even if he wanted to deny it. Luc and Diego had never hidden their sexual preferences. They'd walked into Maris saying "here we are, take us or leave us." They didn't have family or roots here. They'd built every single friendship they'd made with the people who could accept them for who they were, kinks and all. As for the others, they simply moved on.

And while Jeannette had grown up here, she'd always held herself distant. Been a part of Maris life while being apart. She had been painfully shy. Luc and Diego had pulled her out of her burning house, saved her life and her cat, and fallen in love with her. The family had embraced the relationship because they saw how incredibly happy Jeannette was. The cousin who'd retreated into her shell after her parents' untimely death in a car crash had reemerged, and they had the firefighters to thank for that. And the support and approval of her family had helped some other folks to accept it.

Some.

But not all.

Tyson glanced down at the pier. Harley had slipped off her shoes and was sitting at the end, her feet dangling in the water.

"I'm going swimming with her."

Caleb pounded one fist on the arm of his chair. "Dammit, Ty."

"Are you coming?"

They stared at each other for a long time before Caleb nodded. "Yeah. I am. Is there a plan?"

Tyson shook his head as they descended the stairs. "No. All I know is, I need to kiss her again. Just kiss her."

"*She* plans to be naked."

"Yeah. I might have to talk her out of that part."

"So just a kiss," Caleb said, as if he were trying to convince himself that he could handle that.

Tyson paused briefly. "I just have to see if…"

"I know, man. Me too. So let's see. Maybe we'll get lucky and figure out it was a fluke."

That wasn't going to happen and they both knew it.

When they stepped onto the dock, Harley stood and turned to face them. "Finally. I was starting to think you guys were going to chicken out."

She didn't move to take her clothes off, and Tyson realized that while she'd thrown out the dare to go skinny-dipping, she was hesitant too. They were teetering on the edge of a cliff, and it appeared each was cognizant of that fact, and hoping to come out of this unscathed.

"Leave your bra and panties on," Caleb said.

She tilted her head curiously, but didn't refuse.

Tyson decided to take the bull by the horns, stripping off his shirt and then dropping his lounge pants. He stood in front of her in just his boxers, and there was no hiding his erection.

He groaned softly when her gaze lingered south and she licked her lips. "Wow," she whispered, not bothering to pretend she wasn't enjoying the view.

"Great," Caleb muttered. "You're as bad as Tyson."

She laughed. "Is that what took you so long? Debating the wisdom of this?"

Caleb nodded.

"And what was the verdict?"

"Apart from the fact we're all screwed?" Caleb asked.

Harley's grin grew. Tyson had to hand it to the woman. Despite the awkwardness of the situation, she still found the humor in it. "Yeah. Apart from that."

"We both want to kiss you again. *Just* kiss you," Caleb added, stressing that was all.

She appeared to ponder that—and then she reached for the hem of her T-shirt. "Okay, but I should tell you now," she added as she lifted her shirt. "I'm not wearing a bra. Or panties."

Harley turned just as she was getting to the good part, glancing over her shoulder at them with a grin that was half-mischievous and half-sexy as hell, so that they could only see her bare back. She dropped the boxers, giving them a too-brief view of her perfect ass before she dove into the water.

He and Caleb stood there gaping like a couple of fish out of water. Then Tyson shrugged, dropped his own boxers, and walked to the edge.

"Look on the bright side, Cal. That water's going to be frigid. Might help."

Tyson heard Caleb mutter, "It's not going to help," just before Tyson dove in next to Harley.

Not ten seconds later, there was another splash, and Caleb's head broke the surface a few feet away from him. Harley was treading water nearby, laughing as they both cursed.

The water was fucking freezing.

"Better now?" she asked, splashing them both, before turning and swimming away.

"You get the feeling she's having a lot of fun at our expense?" Caleb asked him.

Tyson nodded. "Yeah. Time to get back some of our own."

He started swimming toward Harley. He didn't have to look around to know that Caleb was right behind him. They caught her at the same time. She squealed when Tyson gripped her ankle, pulling her to a stop. She twisted and tried to tug her foot free, but he held fast.

Caleb circled behind her. Tyson dropped her foot when Harley gasped. Caleb's arms had encircled her, resting just below her breasts.

"What's your hurry, Kitten?" Rather than wait for an answer, Caleb placed his lips on her neck and kissed it.

"You've been teasing us this morning, Harley." Tyson was suddenly glad they'd followed her into the water. It would be harder for any of them to dodge the conversation, to walk or swim away if it got too tough. After two weeks of pretty much avoiding the issue or lying about what they really wanted, Tyson was ready to clear the air.

"You're right," she said, pulling Caleb's arms from her. She moved a couple feet, turning so she could look at both of them. The three of them treaded water only an arm's length away from each other. He and Caleb were taller, which meant they could bounce against the bottom every now and again without going under completely. "I'm sorry about that. I know we said we were going to put the kiss behind us, be adults and all that crap."

Tyson chuckled. "Adulting sucks."

"You're right. It does. Listen, I'm just going to come right out and say it. I can't stop thinking about that day in the barn. About those kisses and…"

"Neither can I," Tyson added, when she started to hesitate, her eyes drifting back toward the dock. He couldn't let her go until they said all the things they'd been too afraid to say when she decided to move in.

"I want more."

It was a simple assertion, but her words hit Tyson like a ton of bricks.

"What do you mean *more*?" Caleb was obviously going to fight this every step of the way.

That might have hurt Tyson, but he knew it wasn't a lack of desire on his friend's part. Caleb was one of the most upright, responsible guys he knew. Sure, he could put down whiskey with the best of them and he told some of the dirtiest jokes Tyson had ever heard, but at the end of the day, Caleb was the guy people went to when they needed help moving or building a shed, and he was never too busy to carry groceries to the car for an elderly lady. Tyson couldn't count the number of times Caleb had stopped to help someone change a flat. Tyson and Harley liked to tease him sometimes about his Boy Scout mentality, but it didn't bother Caleb. Tyson sort of thought he liked the comparison.

The locals came to Tyson when they were sick. And they turned to Caleb when they needed a strong back, support, even financial help.

Caleb was also the poster child for the model son. He'd pushed himself hard the past few months, handling all of his family's business affairs, running the Feed and Seed, picking up medications and making sure his mother had everything she needed to care for his dad as he recovered.

Harley didn't reply to his question. Tyson sensed she wasn't sure how to.

"What do you mean by more, Harley?" Caleb repeated.

His gruff tone had Harley backpedaling. "Never mind. Forget it, Cal. I shouldn't have—"

Tyson reached out and pulled her toward him, kissing away the rest of her words. He wasn't going to keep doing the hokey-pokey with these two—putting one toe in and then pulling it right back out again.

Harley resisted the kiss for about a second, and then she went soft in his arms. She wrapped her hands around his neck. He tugged her closer, her bare breasts pressed tightly against his chest. Tyson wasn't sure how they were remaining above water. He assumed they were floating, as neither of them took the time to breathe. All the air in his body was locked inside his chest as his tongue tangled with hers, his fingers gripped her wet hair and his rigid cock—so much for the cold water—was trapped beneath them, resting against her stomach. It was proof of exactly how much *more* Tyson wanted from her.

Seventeen years later, Tyson reluctantly pulled away. He had been afraid to stop kissing her, afraid this would be his last chance.

While Harley didn't seem reluctant to push things further, Caleb would be hard to convince. And they *had* to convince him.

Because what was happening here wasn't just two people feeling an attraction to each other. This didn't work as a couple. That was the strangest part of the whole damn thing. He and Harley wouldn't work without Caleb.

Tyson didn't understand why that was true. He only knew it was.

Harley's hands loosened from around his neck, but remained on his shoulders, resting there. Her dark eyes studied his. They were too serious. She knew what was at stake as well.

"It wasn't a fluke," Tyson said, more for Caleb than Harley, though Harley was the one to answer.

"No. It wasn't. Probably would be easier if it had been."

Caleb remained silent through the entire exchange. Tyson

knew his friend was watching, but he was hesitant to look at him. One glance would tell him what Caleb was thinking—and Tyson couldn't handle it if his friend continued to reject this.

"You're both insane," Caleb muttered, just before he grasped Harley's hand and took his turn.

Tyson couldn't quite understand how watching Caleb and Harley kiss was almost as hot as actually kissing her himself, but he gave them a few minutes before he moved closer. Harley shuddered when Tyson placed his hands on her waist, sliding them along her slick skin down to her hips and back up. His dick was throbbing, hard. Every now and then, it hit her ass.

When the kiss ended, Caleb jerked his head toward the dock. "Come on. This water is freezing. And we all need to put some clothes on before things get out of hand. We're nowhere near finished with this conversation."

Neither Tyson nor Harley disagreed, so the three of them swam for the dock. After climbing the ladder, they quietly put their clothes back on, the material sticking to their wet skin. They hadn't bothered to bring towels.

Caleb claimed the spot on the edge of the dock where Harley had been sitting earlier. He gestured for them to join him. Tyson sat first, and then Harley sank down between them.

"So we kissed again." Caleb wasn't looking at them as he spoke.

"Yeah," Harley added. "We did."

"I want to *keep* kissing you, Harley," Tyson admitted, deciding someone had to get the ball rolling, start saying the hard stuff.

Caleb snorted. "To what end?"

Tyson restated the same thing Caleb had already rejected. "Threesomes aren't exactly unheard of, Cal. Not even in Maris."

"Are you fucking kidding me, Ty? I told you, that can't work."

"Why not?" Harley asked. "Jeannette is living with two guys."

"That's different," Caleb replied. "Luc and Diego…"

Suddenly Tyson understood another reason why Caleb considered Jeannette's ménage lifestyle different from their situation.

"Luc and Diego are lovers too," Tyson finished.

Harley's eyes widened. "Oh."

Caleb snorted. "Yeah. Oh. Besides, those guys also had a long history of dating women together before hooking up with Jeannette. It's *their* kink. Not ours. You and me, Ty—we fly solo. Always have. We're not threesome guys."

Harley giggled, the reaction completely out of place amidst what had devolved into a very tense conversation.

"This conversation sort of reminds me of that *Seinfeld* episode where Jerry considers sleeping with his girlfriend and her roommate. 'I'm not an orgy guy,'" she mimicked.

Tyson chuckled, but Caleb didn't. "You're not taking this seriously, Harl."

"I'm sorry. Honestly, I am taking it seriously, but, well, it's kind of easier to joke about it. I mean, I know how preposterous this is. I just can't shake the feeling that this could work. *Really* work."

"You need to consider all the shit that's going to hit the fan if," Caleb paused, then reconsidered his wording, "*when* people find out."

Harley's eyes widened. "You're considering it."

Caleb didn't bother to deny it. And knowing that his friend wasn't dismissing it out of hand set Tyson's mind at ease. But at the same time, it freaked him out. Because Caleb wasn't wrong. There would be hell to pay if they let this play out the way they were thinking.

"I think it should be an *if* for now." Tyson respected Harley's comments, but, like Caleb, he understood what they were considering was dangerous. And not just to their reputations, which seemed to be Caleb's main concern.

Tyson actually saw a bigger picture, saw how much more they were risking. The friendship. Their hearts. "We've shared two kisses and confirmed we're not *orgy guys*." His joke landed, and he was relieved when both Harley and Caleb laughed. "I think the three of us need to take things slow, see where this leads, see if we can make something work before we start broadcasting it to the world."

"I agree," Harley said. "I mean, let's face it—you guys might totally suck in bed."

Caleb wrapped his arm around Harley's neck, ruffling her hair. "One of these days, you're going to figure out it's never a good idea to dare us."

Harley managed to break free of Caleb's grip, laughing as she stood and backed away from them. "I'm pretty sure if that day was coming, it would have hit already." She looked at them nervously. "So we just roll with it for now?"

Caleb fingered-combed his wet hair. "Yeah."

Harley glanced back toward the house. "What's next?"

"You really do need a plan, don't you, darlin'?" Caleb teased as he rose.

"I'm trying that spirit thing. Honest. I think I might get a shower. Wash off the lake."

"A shower sounds good." Tyson immediately imagined her in the shower…with him scrubbing her back. His tone clearly gave him away.

"Thought we were taking it slow?" Caleb sighed heavily. "Giving ourselves some time to think about it before we roll too far? Before we jump in with both feet? I don't think it's such a bad idea for us to take a few days to think things through. There's a lot of history between us. A lot to lose."

Tyson stood corrected. Caleb saw the big picture too.

"I think that's a good idea." Harley started up the path to the house and they followed.

Tyson revised his shower plan. Now it was just going to be quick, lonely and—given the way his cock refused to say die—cold. "Fine. Maybe after we get cleaned up, we can practice the wedding song."

"What is it?" she asked. "You never said."

"'I Don't Dance'. We've never played it before," Tyson replied.

"Oh. I love that song."

Tyson grinned. "Yeah. And it's pretty perfect for Chas and Syd. You know how much he hates parties and being the center of attention. The fact that she talked him into a big-ass wedding instead of just eloping—which he would have gone for big time—sort of says it all. She's got him wrapped around her finger."

Harley's phone had just stopped ringing when they reached the deck. She walked over to where she'd left it on the arm of the Adirondack and glanced at the screen. "Damn. Four missed calls."

"Who from?" Caleb asked.

"One from Granddad, two from my mom, and…" She paused. "That's weird. One from Art. He never calls me."

Tyson opened the screen door before looking back at her. "Maybe you should call them back. See what's happening. Might be an emergency."

"Yeah," she said distractedly. "I will."

As she dialed and reclaimed her chair on the deck, he and Caleb went into the house to shower and change. He expected Caleb to continue the conversation about what came next— after all, Tyson had gone against everything they'd agreed on. But Caleb simply walked to his room.

When Tyson returned to the living room ten minutes later, Harley was now inside, but still in her damp clothes, arguing with someone on the phone.

"Listen, I don't have to tell you a damn thing." She pulled the phone away from her ear, her gaze flying heavenward as if she was praying for patience.

She hadn't seen him return to the room.

"Who's she talking to?" Caleb murmured behind him.

Tyson shrugged.

Harley placed the phone back to her ear and turned to face them, her exasperated face giving Tyson a clue.

"I'm guessing Art. He's the only person I know who pisses her off that much."

"That guy's such an asshole," Caleb said.

Harley's tone was laced with exasperation. And anger. "Maybe you should just take a hint and back off. If she's not answering the phone, it's probably because she doesn't want to talk to you. We've been down this road before."

Yep. It was Art.

"No. I'm not going to tell her to call you."

It appeared Art wasn't finished making demands when Harley sighed and rubbed her eyes wearily. She'd left town after Johnnie's funeral to escape the drama that constantly surrounded her family.

"It's none of your business if she was at the barn party last night." She paused, then gritted her teeth. "Yes, I'm perfectly aware of how I'm going to burn in hell. Thanks for the reminder."

Tyson's temper piqued. He wasn't going to let Art keep using her as his whipping post, lashing out whenever her mom tried to cut and run. And he wasn't going to let her *mom* keep using Harley, either. The woman was an emotional drain, constantly crying to Harley and expecting her daughter to take care of all her problems for her.

And while Art had never said any of the cruel things he knew the man lobbed in Harley's direction in front of them, she always filled Tyson and Caleb in on the particulars. From the look on Harley's face, the man was in a fury and chewing her out something fierce. God only knew what names he was calling her right now.

When it dragged on a second too long, Tyson walked across the room and plucked the phone out of Harley's hand. "Art, this is Tyson Sparks. I'm only going to tell you this once, so I'm going to need you to listen good. Your marriage is your own business. Stop harassing Harley. Call her again, and you can expect a visit from me where we'll settle this man to man."

He tapped on the screen to end the call as Harley's expression morphed from surprise to pure delight.

"That was sort of awesome."

Tyson's anger hadn't abated. "I don't like the way he yells at you, Harley. If he calls again, let it go to voice mail. Under no circumstances should you answer the phone."

Harley narrowed her eyes as she studied him curiously.

"I mean it, Harley. Don't answer the phone."

Tyson noticed Caleb had dropped down on the couch, his feet resting on the coffee table, crossed at the ankles.

"What?" Tyson asked when they both continued to look at him like he'd suddenly sprouted an extra head.

"Don't look at me," Caleb said when Tyson's gaze returned to him. "I'm just here for the show."

"Show?" Tyson asked.

Harley laughed softly. "Part of me thinks I should be a little pissed off at you for this overly macho routine, but the truth is, it's super hot."

Caleb dropped his feet to the floor and leaned up at that. "Oh yeah? You think that's hot? Because, sugar, I got alpha moves that would knock your socks off."

Tyson blew out an exasperated breath. "Y'all just made *me* dial it back. I took that damn cold shower so I could sit here without a raging hard-on in my pants. So which is it? Time-out or forge on?"

Harley bit her lower lip. "Sorry. I think it's still a time-out. Truth is, I'm kind of worried about my mom. Not sure where she is."

"Did you call her?" Caleb asked.

She nodded. "Yeah. She didn't answer. Neither did Grand-dad. After last night, I'm not sure what to think."

Tyson gave her phone back to her. "What happened last night?"

"I found my dad in Johnnie's room."

"You told us that." Tyson had attributed her silence in the car on the way home to the fact she was missing her brother. Apparently she hadn't been the only one in the family to feel his absence.

"My mom was with him."

Caleb's brows flew up. "Seriously? But they don't speak."

"Ever," Harley said. "I know. She was crying and he was comforting her."

Tyson wasn't sure what to make of that information. Harley's parents had divorced when they were all in tenth grade, and as far as Tyson knew, they hadn't said more than fifty words to each other since. "Wow."

"I think I might head out to the farm just to—"

Her phone rang before she could finish her sentence.

"It's her." Harley answered the phone. "Hey, Mom. Where are you? Why? Um…okay. I won't say anything. Yeah. Okay. Bye."

"Where is she?" Tyson asked.

"At the farm. She spent the night in my room. She asked me not to tell Art."

Caleb stood up and took her hand. "You okay with that?"

Harley gave him a funny look. "I guess. I can't think of why I wouldn't be. It's just really weird."

"There's a lot of that going around," Caleb said as he tugged her toward him for a hug, and then he placed a kiss on the top of her head.

She lifted her head from Caleb's chest so she could see his face. "Like this?"

Caleb sighed. "Nothing about this is weird, which actually makes it the weirdest thing of all."

She giggled. "Yeah. You're right. So, I'm just going to add this new development with my parents to the list of things I'm rolling with. Get your instruments, boys. We need to practice for a wedding."

$\mathscr{C}$aleb rubbed Harley's feet as she lay between him and
Tyson on the couch. It was Friday night after a long
damn week. His dad had a bad reaction to some new medica-
tion on Tuesday, so Caleb had spent two nights at his parents'
house helping his mom out. Tyson had gotten a call in the
middle of the night to deliver a baby on Wednesday, and
between visits to the bank to sort out a loan for her new business and to the farm to visit her mom—who was still there,
Harley hadn't been home much either.

While Caleb had been grateful for the time to consider
what was happening between them, he could have used a little
less of it. Between stressing out over his dad's health and the
whole should we/shouldn't we wrangling, he'd also spent one
too many nights trying to imagine the actual logistics.

Tyson and Harley could joke all they wanted about that
"we're not orgy guys" thing, but the idea of taking off his
clothes and crawling into a bed naked with Harley *and* Tyson
was damn intimidating. He didn't question his skills—he was
probably overly confident when it came to his moves in the

bedroom. But that didn't mean he wanted to perform them in front of another guy. Even if it was just Tyson.

The only thing that alleviated that anxiety was when he recalled watching Harley and Tyson kiss. He sure as hell didn't have the same hang-ups when it came to playing voyeur. He liked watching them. A lot.

He sighed.

"Okay," Harley said, her gaze moving from the TV to his face. "What's wrong? That's the third heavy sigh in the last ten minutes."

Caleb frowned. He hadn't meant to give himself away. "Sorry."

"I thought everything was better with your dad?" Harley's head was resting in Tyson's lap and his friend was playing with her hair absentmindedly.

That was another thing wreaking havoc on him. There had been a definite shift in the physical dynamics between them since Harley had moved in. They stole kisses whenever they could, and in the rare moments when they were all together— like now—the distance between them shrank.

Tyson paused the old movie they'd selected from Netflix. "Thought that new medicine was working?"

"It is," Caleb said. "I was actually thinking about something else."

Tyson gave him a crooked grin. "Guess I don't have to ask what."

"And that's what's making you sigh?" Harley asked. "Us? Honest, Cal, if you think we shouldn't venture into the deep end, then we won't. I don't want a couple of kisses to ruin a lifetime of friendship."

She'd misinterpreted his anxiety. His problem wasn't that

he didn't want to be with her. He wanted her so fucking much it was distracting him from everything else.

"I don't want to ruin it either." Caleb grasped her hands and pulled her up until she was sitting between them, her legs still lying over his lap. He cupped her cheeks, pulling her lips toward his.

It was physically impossible to be so close and not kiss her. Harley didn't hold back either. Their lips opened, their tongues touched. Her hands held tightly to his shoulders as he deepened the kiss.

When they parted, he placed his forehead against hers. "My head tells me this is wrong, but…"

"But it doesn't feel wrong," she finished when he realized he wasn't making this easier for any of them.

He shook his head. "No, it doesn't."

And just like that, everything shifted. Apparently, they'd run out of excuses.

Tyson moved behind Harley, reaching for the hem of her T-shirt. He tugged the cotton over her head.

"What do you have against bras?" Caleb asked, grinning widely.

"I yanked it off as soon as I got home. Always do. Is that a complaint?"

Caleb shook his head as he cupped one of her bare breasts. She was soft and sweet and purred like a kitten in his arms. "Not at all."

Tyson ran his lips along the side of Harley's neck as she looked at Caleb with such desire, such intense need, it took his breath away, fueled his own.

"Whose bedroom?" Caleb had run through the logistics

enough to know he didn't even want to try to make this work on the couch the first time.

"Mine's closer and the bed's bigger," Tyson said as he stood and helped Harley off Caleb's lap. The two of them headed down the hallway, but Caleb didn't move.

Instead, he took a second to suck in some much-needed air. His cock was thick and throbbing. He was ready for this. Too ready.

But while they'd kissed and talked, none of them had truly turned the corner, had started down a path with no hope of returning.

Right now, at this moment, they could call a halt and things could return to normal. Friends forever. Platonic roommates.

After tonight?

Well...

After tonight, everything would change.

"Caleb," Harley called from down the hall.

He stood up, grinning as he walked toward Tyson's room. After too many years of living up to other people's expectations, tonight Caleb was doing something that was just for him. Taking something that he wanted more than anything in his life.

Tonight, he wasn't just going to turn the corner. He was going to cross the bridge, set fire to it, and then leave the damn country.

Tyson and Harley were standing inside the doorway to his friend's bedroom. They were kissing, Tyson's hands cupping her breasts, squeezing them gently.

Caleb leaned on the doorjamb, content to watch as his own arousal, his own hunger grew.

Harley grasped the bottom of Tyson's T-shirt, pulling it off him, her fingers drifting along his chest.

Tyson continued to kiss her, his hands moving, stroking every inch of her he could reach.

"Take off her pants," Caleb demanded.

Tyson released Harley's lips, his hands gripping her waist when it appeared she'd take a step away.

Both of them looked at him, questioningly. His tardiness coming to the room had been noticed. Clearly they thought he was still hesitant.

Nothing could be further from the truth.

"Take off her pants, Ty. *Now.*"

The concern in Tyson's gaze cleared as he stepped behind Harley, giving Caleb an unobstructed view of their soon-to-be lover.

Harley started to lift her hands to cover her breasts, uncharacteristically shy under his intense scrutiny.

He shook his head, just once, and she found her confidence once more and let her hands fall to her sides again.

Tyson worked the elastic of her lounge pants over her hips. It was instantly obvious it wasn't just the bra she'd shed earlier.

"No panties," Caleb remarked with a grin.

She shrugged unapologetically.

The cotton pants dropped to the floor once they cleared her hips and she kicked them off.

"Goddamn. You're so beautiful, love."

Harley hadn't blushed at her nudity, but her cheeks went pink at Caleb's praise. Then he considered something he hadn't thought of before.

"How long has it been for you, Harley?"

There hadn't been anyone at home since she'd broken up with Juan years earlier. But that didn't mean she hadn't met someone in Florida.

Then she confirmed what he already knew. "Not since Juan."

"Jesus," Tyson muttered. "Talk about diving off the deep end. No sex in years and now…"

"I'm a champ when it comes to masturbating," she joked.

Caleb laughed. Tyson didn't. He also didn't say what they were all thinking. She was going from cold turkey to ménage in the blink of an eye.

"We'll go slow," Tyson whispered against her neck.

While his friend couldn't see Harley's unspoken response to that comment, Caleb had a front row seat to her expressions.

She didn't want slow. If anything, the abstinence was taking its toll on her.

"Or," Caleb said, walking to stand in front of her. "We'll go hard and fast and kinky as hell. Preference?"

She laughed breathlessly. "What you said sounds good."

Tyson lifted his head, glancing at Caleb's face. His friend instantly understood he'd misread her needs. "Get on the bed, Harley."

Caleb took the time to enjoy the view of her ass as she climbed into the middle of Tyson's king-size mattress. Even with the large bed, they'd be a tight fit. Neither he nor Tyson were small men.

If Tyson was feeling any of the same reticence that had been lingering in Caleb's mind all week, he didn't show it. His lounge pants joined Harley's on the floor within seconds, and then Tyson was beside her on the mattress, kissing her once more.

While he enjoyed the show, Caleb figured it was time to catch the hell up. He stripped quickly and climbed onto the bed on the opposite side.

When the mattress sank under his weight, Tyson released her, so she could turn and give him some of those oh-so-sweet kisses.

Caleb closed his eyes, savoring the feeling of her hands on his shoulders, and her soft mews whenever he deepened the kiss, or when…

Caleb's eyelids slid open as he pulled away briefly. Tyson's hands had slipped around her, cupping her breasts, toying with the nipples. Caleb watched Tyson play with her, observed her response to the touches—sometimes soft, sometimes a bit rougher.

Everything in his life fell into place.

God, now that he was here, it seemed so damn obvious.

He'd been in love with Harley forever and he didn't even realize it. What's more, he loved Tyson too. He craved his friend's presence in the bed as much as he longed to bury himself deep inside Harley's body.

Caleb reached lower, rubbing just one finger between her legs, seeking her clit.

Harley gasped softly, then spread her legs apart, granting him easier access. The motion was the equivalent to firing a starter's pistol at the beginning of a race.

Tyson gently pressed Harley to her back between them. As Caleb ran his fingers along her slit, Tyson leaned closer, sucking one of her nipples into his mouth.

Harley's hips tilted toward his touch, silently demanding

more. He wasn't about to refuse that request. Caleb slid two fingers inside. She was warm, tight, wet. Perfect.

"Oh my God," she whispered on a breath.

Tyson lifted his head, looking down at Caleb's fingers slipping in and out. He'd started slow, but her breathless cries for more, the way her hips were thrusting in time, drove him to move faster.

Her whole body jerked when Tyson joined the party down under, rubbing her clit until she cried out louder.

"I need…" she gasped. "Need…"

Tyson looked at him.

Moment of truth.

"You first," Caleb said.

Tyson reached into the nightstand and pulled out two condoms. He tossed one to Caleb before putting his own on.

Harley had stilled, her eyes drifting between them. She was breathing heavily. They hadn't pushed her over the edge, so her orgasm remained, simmering just beneath the surface.

"You okay, darlin'?" Caleb asked.

She nodded.

He lay next to her as Tyson knelt between her outstretched legs. Both of them watched as he directed his cock to her opening and then as it slowly disappeared inside.

Caleb hadn't put his own condom on yet, so he wrapped his fist around his cock, stroking it in time with Tyson's movements.

Harley caught sight of his actions, reaching out to take the task over. Her grip was light, tentative. So Caleb covered her hand with his as Tyson continued to take her slowly.

All three of them were aware of everything that was happening in that bed. While he and Harley watched Tyson's cock disappear, then reappear, Tyson's gaze rested on Harley and Caleb's hand stroking his dick.

For a few moments, the pace remained slow, steady. Then, as their arousal grew, so did their need for more. Tyson began to press in harder, faster, and Caleb matched his grip—and Harley's—to their rhythm.

Soon they were all breathing heavily, Harley crying out as her climax inched ever closer.

Tyson bent lower to place a kiss on her cheek. "God, Harley. I'm so close."

"Me. Too." She forced the words out.

Caleb tugged her hand away from his cock. He was too damn close himself and there was no way he wasn't coming inside her body this first time. He held her hand, gritting his teeth as her grip tightened. Her back arched off the mattress as she came, Tyson there as well, jerking with the force of his own climax.

Despite just coming, both Harley and Tyson seemed to be perfectly aware of Caleb's presence and the fact he was still hurting.

Tyson withdrew slowly, the action provoking a powerful shudder in Harley's body. He dropped down to her side, clearing the path for Caleb.

Caleb bent closer to her, kissing her just once. "You okay, gorgeous?"

She smiled sweetly. "I will be once you hurry your ass up and get inside me."

Game, set, match.

His heart belonged to Harley Mills, and it would until the day he died.

He quickly slid the condom on and within seconds, he was pushing his way into paradise.

Harley wrapped her ankles around his waist. He considered giving her time to recover from her previous orgasm, but he recalled her face when Tyson promised her slow. Then he remembered her responses to their rougher touches.

They'd never held back with Harley, telling her all their tales, including her in all their locker room talk.

Her eyes locked with his and he knew she remembered the stories too.

"Do it," she prodded.

Caleb let go of the reins, took her the way he loved. Fast, hard. He liked the slightest bit of pain with his pleasure, something he'd confessed to his best friends several years earlier.

He'd noticed then that they hadn't been shocked or appalled. In fact, if he'd had his freaking eyes open, he would have recognized the same desires in them.

Caleb reached for one of her breasts, pinching her nipple with some serious pressure.

Harley jerked and her pussy clenched tightly against his dick.

Tyson reached for her face—the doctor in him doing what came natural, checking to make sure she was okay. "Harley?"

She grinned. "I think we're going to get really good at this...and by good, I mean super dirty."

Caleb laughed, even as he continued to thrust inside her. "God, I love you two."

As far as pronouncements went, that one came too soon.

And too late.

Tyson's brows lifted with humor. "Never thought Cal would be the sappy one."

Caleb stilled his motions, shooting his best friend a dirty look, though there was no real heat behind it.

Harley giggled. Then she reached out to cup each of their cheeks. "I love you guys too. Still screwed?" she asked Caleb.

He nodded. "Oh, hell yeah. But if we're going down, I say we do it in a blaze of glory."

Caleb thrust in once, more roughly than before. Then twice, three times more. Tyson reached between their bodies, stroking her clit.

Harley closed her eyes tightly, gasping for air. And then, without a single word, they both let go. At the exact same time.

Caleb fell to her side. Tyson was propped up on his elbow looking at the two of them as they struggled to catch their breath.

None of them spoke for a few minutes. No doubt his friends were trying to let what just happened soak in. God knew that was what *he* was doing.

Harley, ever the brave one, broke the silence first. "Regrets?"

"No." Tyson's reply came instantly.

Caleb shook his head, but his reply took a second too long. "No."

Harley's gaze slid his way. "Say what's on your mind, Cal."

There wasn't anything he couldn't say to these two. Sometimes he thought they knew him better than he knew himself. "I was raised in a pretty strict household by ultra-conservative parents. Everything I've ever been taught by my parents would tell me that what we just did was wrong. Really wrong."

Harley bit her lip, her eyes troubled. "You said you don't have regrets."

"That's just it. I don't. This isn't wrong. I have no fucking idea how I'll convince my parents of that, but that doesn't mean I'm not going to try. Or that I'm going to let their beliefs stop me from grabbing this."

Tyson grinned. "Welcome aboard. You realize you were trying to convince me we should miss this trip. Just stay safe on shore."

Caleb reached across Harley's body to punch his friend on the shoulder. "Okay, metaphor man. You want to play that way? You're right. The cruise is awesome. But a hurricane is heading right for us. You ready for that?"

Tyson shrugged. "We're thirty-two years old, Cal. Don't you think that's too fucking old to be worrying so much about what people think that we deny ourselves true happiness?" Tyson glanced down at Harley. "And love."

"I get that. But I love my folks, respect them, and—for better or worse—I do care about their opinion. Jesus, my dad just had a heart attack and his health is tenuous at best. Finding out I'm sleeping with you and Harley could push him over the edge."

Tyson didn't reply to that. Caleb knew it was because, while Tyson was completely in as far as this relationship was concerned, he felt the same way about *his* family. Tyson wanted his dad's approval and respect as much as Caleb did. They'd both grown up idolizing their fathers. And while it was easy to say to hell with it, this is right and what makes me happy and I don't give a shit what others say, it was another thing completely to actually walk that walk.

"We could lay low with this if you want." Harley was sweet

to make the offer, but neither Caleb nor Tyson were fans of deception or lying.

"You think this will get old? That we'll figure out it was a mistake somewhere down the line?" Caleb asked Harley.

She shook her head. "I hope we can make it work forever."

Caleb kissed her on the cheek. "So do I. And if it was just you and me, I'd be taking you out for dinner tomorrow night, holding your hand, kissing you in public and making damn sure every guy in town knew you were mine."

She smiled somewhat sadly. "I like the sound of that. But I don't need it. We can just keep up the roommate pretense for…"

"For how long?" Tyson asked. "How long would you all be willing to hide your true feelings?"

"I don't want to hide," Caleb said. Despite his concerns for his family, he hated the idea of lying to them even more. "Hiding insinuates that we're doing something wrong. We're not."

"Fine," Harley said. "So we'll come out slowly. Tell our families and close friends first, and only when we're able to. Until then, we just keep the hand-holding and kissing private. There's no huge rush. I mean…let's face it…this is brand spanking new. We should probably try to come to grips with it ourselves first."

"Okay," Caleb agreed. They did need to take some time to figure out how and when they'd break the news. Until then, he didn't want to ruin what was shaping up to being the best night of his life.

"So who's ready for round two?" Tyson asked.

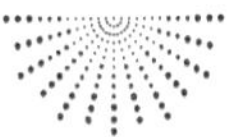

$\mathcal{H}$arley spun around the store and resisted the urge to pinch herself. Since returning home, it felt almost as if she were living a dream. A really racy dream.

She smiled when she recalled the past ten days. She, Caleb and Tyson hadn't needed to worry about coming out to anyone because they'd found it damn hard to leave the house. No, scratch that. It was the bedroom they were struggling to leave.

While Caleb and Tyson went to work each day, they kept their hours as short as possible, rushing back home to her. During the days, when they were gone, she did a lot of research online in terms of stocking her music store and the million other things associated with starting a business from the ground up.

This past weekend, they'd only managed to leave the bedroom for food occasionally, and twice they'd walked down to the lake at dusk to go skinny-dipping. Unlike their first foray into naked swimming, the second two attempts were enough to bring the chilly lake water to a boil.

Now that they'd made the leap from friends to lovers, Caleb and Tyson seemed happier, more easygoing. At least, they did when they were in the privacy of their own home. Today was her first day out in the real world with them, and Harley was anxious, nervous to see what would transpire. They'd basically agreed to tell people at their own pace. If it were up to her, she would have walked through town with a megaphone this morning, screaming it to everyone who would listen.

After so many years of just existing, Harley felt like she'd finally woken up, come to life. She was in love. When she considered her previous relationship with Juan, she realized this was the first time she'd ever felt this way. It was amazing, incredible, heavenly.

"You're going to have to practice wiping that smile off your face or you'll give us all away without having to say a word," Caleb said, wrapping his arm around her shoulder and giving her a quick kiss on the top of her head. Both he and Tyson had her by at least half a foot. Vertically challenged, they liked to tease her. She'd never felt that disparity in size until they flanked her in bed. Her own personal, muscly man cave. She loved nestling beneath them, loved how secure, how protected she felt. Harley could happily hibernate underneath her fellas for the rest of her life.

Caleb placed a strong finger beneath her chin, lifting her face up. He narrowed his eyes playfully. "And now you're blushing. You really need to work on your poker face, hot stuff."

"Sorry. I'll try harder."

Caleb looked as if he didn't have much confidence in her success. Of course, he looked a lot like the cat who ate the canary himself, so she wasn't the only one giving them away. Not that it mattered here.

They were alone in Jill's old beauty shop. The former renter had cleared out the place this weekend, while Harley had been rolling around in bed with the landlord. Typically, Bugsy, the property manager, would have been the tour guide, showing Harley the space, but Caleb had insisted on coming with her instead.

They'd stopped by Bugsy's office to grab the key before heading here. Bugsy never questioned why Caleb was taking the lead on this rental. For one, everyone in town knew Caleb and Harley were close friends, and secondly, Caleb had shared Harley's plans for the property and his vested interest in the business.

Given that the Hott family owned at least half the town, no one would blink twice at Caleb investing in yet another venture. Especially not one that included her and music.

"So what do you think?" Caleb asked, gesturing at the space. "What was your plan for the layout of the store?"

Harley reached into her pocket and withdrew a sketch she'd made last Thursday after he and Tyson had gone to work. This morning, Tyson had taken off early to head into Douglas to do some rounds at the hospital, which left her and Caleb alone to get ready. Caleb had tried to entice her into the shower with him, but Harley had resisted, knowing that if she agreed, neither of them would make it to town today. Plus, Tyson would have been pissed off to miss out on all the fun.

Harley still wasn't sure *how* this thing between them was working. Or why. But she didn't want to test too many boundaries until they'd had time to talk out a few things. Very few words had been spoken about the particulars of what they were embarking on, and how it would work, as they lost themselves in the newness, the excitement of what they'd discovered.

However, there were quite a few conversations lined up on the docket. And until they happened, Harley wasn't about to upset the apple cart.

"Here." She handed him the paper, a bit nervous as he studied her crude drawing. Caleb had studied business in college, earning an MBA at Texas A&M. Harley's retail resume consisted of only one year's worth of experience garnered at her great-aunt's beachside shop.

"This is really good, Harl."

She wanted to be relieved by his comment, but she couldn't get past the slight tone of amazement in his voice. "Surprised?"

He gave her a sheepish grin. "No?"

She rolled her eyes. "Asshole."

"It's a solid setup, sweetheart. Seriously. You've really got a good eye in terms of layout and making the best use of the space. Tempted to have you come over to the Feed and Seed and give me some feedback on how to fix *that* place. After forty years in business, the thing is a hodgepodge. We add a new product and the goal becomes simply finding a place for it, rather than finding the best place. I'm starting to get claustrophobic there."

She agreed with the claustrophobic atmosphere of the Feed and Seed. "Not sure I'd have a clue how to help. That place is a maze. Besides, while it feels like craziness to you, you have to consider your customers. Very few people more set in their ways than farmers. You go moving everything around and they'll flip out."

Caleb grimaced and sighed. "Yeah. I know. I think that's why I'm excited about this place. We can take the time to do it right."

She loved it when he said "we." While she had expected to feel the grief she'd experienced after Johnnie's death, what took her down harder was the sudden loneliness. Her brother had been her closest companion her entire life—always there, always listening. In Florida, she hadn't had anyone to confide her deepest secrets to.

This weekend, as the three of them lay in bed together, Harley found all her thoughts, hopes, dreams and fears spilling out of her. And the loneliness had vanished. Instantly.

"I thought we could use this space back here for the music lessons," she said, walking toward the rear of the store.

For the next hour, they discussed what instruments she would stock, discussed sheet music options and, as Harley did some quick searches on her phone, they looked at shelving.

"Damn," Caleb said, glancing at his watch. "I was supposed to be at the Feed and Seed twenty minutes ago." He handed her the key. "Why don't you keep looking around and then lock the place up behind you? We can start making some to-do lists tonight at dinner when Tyson's around to offer some input. The countdown to opening up shop starts now."

"God. That's exciting as hell. And completely terrifying. I only need a couple more minutes here. I just want to get a few more measurements for the storage closets and then I'm heading over to the bank to sign the final papers on the loan. Once that's done, I'll get with Bugsy to discuss the lease."

Caleb winked. "Sounds like a plan, Stan."

She laughed, reaching up on tiptoe to steal a quick kiss. Or at least that had been her intention. Caleb clearly had other plans.

He wrapped his arms around her back and held her in place, pressing her lips open so he could steal a taste. Harley ran her fingers through his hair, savoring this sudden closeness.

After endless hours—days—of touching and kissing, Harley found herself hungrier for more rather than sated. How long would it take before she was fully satisfied? Something told her years. A lifetime.

Caleb tugged her closer, letting her feel his erection against her stomach. While they were toward the back of the store, that didn't mean anyone walking past couldn't look in the large plate glass window and see them.

Harley pulled away, her mouth a mere inch or two from Caleb's. "Guess there's no chance you could skip work today? We could swing by Tyson's office, force him to cancel all his appointments and go back home."

Caleb placed a gentle kiss to her forehead. "That's the most tempting offer I've ever had in my life."

"And yet you still have to say no. More of that adulting stuff?"

He nodded. "Afraid so."

They kissed once more, this one with less heat, but by no means less exciting.

"Shit," Caleb muttered as they moved apart.

"That bad?" she joked.

He shook his head. "Your stepdad is outside watching us. He saw the kiss."

Harley glanced over just in time to catch Art's disapproving scowl. "Shit," she said, repeating Caleb's sentiment. "Maybe it just looked like a friendly kiss."

Caleb tilted his head in a "seriously?" manner and she knew he was right. The first kiss had been molten and the second had definitely been overly affectionate, bordering on romantic. She had no idea how long Art had been there, but even if he'd only caught the tail end, he'd seen too much.

"Art wasn't the first person I wanted to start with," Harley murmured.

Caleb grinned. "Yeah. You're not kidding. Judgmental prick. But I think we can dodge this one. Say Art didn't have a clear view and he was mistaken, or hell, it wouldn't make me feel too guilty to call the guy a liar outright."

"His dislike for me is pretty well known. It wouldn't be out of the realm of believability for him to try to start a rumor about us. Besides, there aren't too many people who like Art. Most folks around here tune him out."

Harley understood there were a lot of reasons for keeping quiet as well beyond the risk of hurting their families.

There weren't many times she'd actually felt fortunate to have such a fucked-up family, but the fact that her parents had screwed up their own lives so royally basically meant they didn't exactly have high expectations for her success in romance either.

Granddad might be shocked at first, but he loved Tyson and Caleb like they were his own, and she'd heard him remark a couple times now about how sweet he thought Jeannette's relationship with the firefighters was. Now that she considered it, she wondered if she had somehow shown her hand, and he was telling her that he was cool with whatever might transpire between her and the guys.

Caleb and Tyson had more to lose than she did—their standing in the community, as well as the potential loss of business and patients.

"I need to hit the road. See you at home in a few?"

She nodded, wishing he could give her one last kiss good-bye, but it was clear by the determination on his face, Caleb didn't intend to make the same mistake again.

Harley waved as he left, then went back to the storage closet to record the measurements on her paper. She wanted to feel excited about the prospect of the new store and her future plans, but that feeling was muted by her concerns over what that same future held for Caleb and Tyson.

"What are you doing in here?"

Harley jumped at the sound of a man's voice behind her. She turned and tried not to grimace when she spotted Art in the doorway of the storage closet. Fucker had her trapped.

"I'm renting this place."

She wasn't going to give him any more details than that. The man had never approved of anything she'd done. At the beginning of Art's marriage to her mom, Harley had tried to forge a relationship with the man, tried to please him by attending church with the two of them, spending the occasional weekend at their house. And at first, it was okay. Sort of.

However, neither Harley nor Art managed to play nice for long. She had been right in the midst of her teen years, which meant rebellion was her middle name. Throw in a self-righteous, overly critical stepfather and Harley had worked over-time to make sure Art was unhappy by pushing every single one of his buttons.

She'd like to say she regretted her actions back then, but as more years passed, it had become abundantly clear that Art was a genuinely bad person. Not just to her and her mom, but to everyone. He had exactly three friends, equally as judgmental and miserable as him. They fed on each other like a cancer.

"Renting it? What for?"

"What do you want, Art?"

"Saw you kissing Caleb. Thought you were going out with the doctor."

Fuck. He *had* seen too much.

"What made you think I was dating Tyson?"

"That phone call the other day. I don't appreciate being threatened."

"It's clear the threat fell on deaf ears. We have nothing to talk about, Art."

Art scoffed. "Yeah. Right. Your mother filed for divorce this morning."

Harley worked overtime to keep her face impassive. In truth, she was shocked as hell. Her mother had never made a single move on her own without Harley hearing about it. Jesus, her mother actually never made a move at all. She generally told Harley what she wanted and Harley did the legwork, tried to find a way to give her what she wanted. Typically, that meant moving her mom out of Art's house. She had never gotten her mom as far as a lawyer's office. The fact that her mother did this without her...without even telling her...

Harley couldn't decide if she was relieved or hurt.

God, talk about old habits dying hard. It was well past time her mom took care of herself, and Harley was glad to know she was doing that.

"So?" Her nonchalant tone appeared to fool Art. Not that it would take much to fool him. Art knew who'd been pulling the strings on all her mother's failed attempts to escape over the years.

Art had done quite a number on Mom's self-esteem. Harley had read an article once about bullying behavior and emotional abuse. Art's techniques were textbook.

"So I want to know where she is. She's not returning my calls."

"This conversation is starting to feel a lot like déjà vu. After all these years, it's like you don't know me at all."

"Determined to ruin my marriage, aren't you? Not that I should be surprised. You never did have any morals. Heard you moved in with Caleb and Tyson. Living in sin with two men! There's a word for women like you."

Harley laughed. "Let me guess. Whore? Slut? Which one were you leaning toward today? Or maybe you were thinking of something fancier. Jezebel? I always liked it when you used that one. Felt like you were making a real effort."

"If the shoe fits..."

"Apparently it fits me like a glove," she taunted, making sure he knew how little his insults hurt her. When she was sixteen, she'd made the mistake of crying when he'd embarrassed her in front of some girlfriends, telling her only a whore would show so much of her body when she'd worn a bikini in public. She'd been at the beach by the lake and had expected her mother to come pick her up. Instead, Art showed up, storming across the sand, demanding that she wrap herself in a towel and get in the car. It was the first time he'd called her a slut. And it had hurt like hell.

When they returned home, he'd dragged her mother—

who'd gone to bed with a blinding migraine—downstairs and told both of them they were sinners. Harley for wearing the bikini and her mother for allowing it. Then he'd told them to get on their knees and pray for forgiveness.

It was the first time Harley defied Art. She'd refused. And he'd slapped her.

Harley had looked at her mother, expecting her to defend her, to get them out of the house. Instead, her mother had knelt to pray.

Harley had run out of the house and straight home. Granddad and Johnnie had comforted her, and then her grandfather had paid a visit to Art. Harley had no idea what had been said between the men, but that had been the last time she'd ever stayed in Art's house.

"I *will* find her, Harley. And when I do, she's coming home. Where she belongs. Divorce is a sin."

So it was the divorce he was worried about. Not his wife. Harley's blood boiled, but she didn't bother to respond. She'd learned a long time ago her silence was just as powerful as words with Art. He loved to argue, so when she shut up and offered him nothing to respond to, he got frustrated.

"You hear me?"

She just stared at him, stone-faced.

"You tell Polly that I expect her home tonight! Hiding from me isn't going to get her what she wants."

Harley didn't move, barely blinked. She just painted on her best bored look and held it.

Art turned and stormed out of the storage closet, his last word his usual goodbye. "Whore," he muttered as he left the store, forcefully shoving the front door open. No doubt he would have slammed it if he could have.

Harley sucked in a breath. She needed to calm down, but right now, she was overwhelmed by the desire to punch something. Hard.

"Fuck it," she said aloud to the room. "Fuck *him*."

She took her measurements, wrote them down, and then she left. She wasn't in the mood to dream about her new store anymore. Between Art and her mother, and concern over Tyson's and Caleb's reputations, she decided fresh air and a nice long walk were in order.

Locking the door behind her, she tucked the key in her pocket and headed for the park. There was a lovely walking path through the trees that had always been one of her favorite retreats. Many a Wednesday, she'd drop Johnnie off at Sparks Barbeque and then head off to the park for a long walk, while her brother flirted with Macie.

The memory didn't make her as sad as she might have imagined. She missed Johnnie, but as more time passed, that feeling lessened. She knew it would never go away completely, but at least now, the pain was more manageable.

She walked for a good hour and the solitude of the place worked its magic on her. Grabbing a bench in a particularly secluded spot, she dropped down and glanced up. It was a picture-perfect day. The sky was bright blue with fluffy, white clouds and soft sunlight. There was a cool breeze blowing that kept the humidity at bay.

She sighed contentedly as she closed her eyes and enjoyed the warmth of the sun on her face.

When she opened her eyes again, a movement to her right caught her attention.

It was clear her father was as surprised to find her here as she was to see him. But they were too close to ignore the fact they'd both seen the other.

Her dad only hesitated for a moment and then he continued toward her. Looked like today was her day for uncomfortable confrontations.

When he was close, he gestured toward the spot next to her. "Mind if I join you?"

She shook her head and slid over to make room.

Dad sat down, but his eyes remained forward, focusing on the trees across the path from them. "I like this place."

She didn't bother to look at him. This was the first time her father had attempted to have a real conversation with her since before Johnnie's death. "Me too."

"You know it wasn't always a park. Back when I was in high school, this was actually the edge of town. A lot of these paths were dirt lanes through the trees. I used to wait for your mom after school. She'd hop on the back of my motorcycle and we'd ride all over this place. I didn't have my Harley back then, just a piece of shit Honda I'd gotten secondhand from a guy in Douglas."

It had never been any secret Harley's name had come from her dad's beloved Harley-Davidson. And Johnnie's from the Johnnie Walker whiskey he loved…a bit little before they were born and too fucking much after Johnnie was confined to the chair. Shortly after Johnnie's accident, she'd viewed their names as curses. However, before that, she'd always loved them, thought they were unique and special.

She'd been a daddy's girl until the accident, certain that her father hung the moon. That feeling had faded over the years until she'd all but forgotten the man who'd taught her how to ride a horse, fish, and skip stones in the lake.

He pointed out a particularly dense copse. "Polly and I used to park over there and…well, you know." He let his wink and grin fill in the rest.

Harley couldn't help but answer his smile with one of her own. It had been a long time since she'd seen that easy grin on his face. "I didn't know that." Then she jokingly added, "And I really don't need to know any *more* than that." It was hard enough to reconcile the parents who barely acknowledged each other's presence with the two people she'd seen in Johnnie's room the other night. It would be impossible to add in any component that involved them being in love and having sex.

"Your mom used to call me her bad boy."

Given his love of whiskey, tattoos, motorcycles and loud rock music, Harley figured that description was accurate. Which made her mother's second marriage to the most boring, devout, straight-laced man on the planet make a bit more sense.

And no sense at all.

If she was looking for polar opposites, Mom had found them in Dad and Art.

"Guess she was right," he murmured, more to himself than to her.

Harley glanced over, looking at him—really looking—for the first time in a long time. Years spent abusing alcohol had taken their toll. When she was younger, she'd always thought her daddy was the most handsome man in Maris. The lines around his eyes were grooved deeper than they used to be, the wrinkles not driven by the smile that always used to be on his face, but rather by stress.

When she left last year, he'd been sporting a large spare

tire, a serious beer gut. Obviously Granddad had worked that extra weight off him at the farm. He was slimmer now, and the muscles he had used to lift her on one shoulder and Johnnie on the other when they were kids were starting to reappear.

An ancient tattoo peeked beneath the edge of his T-shirt sleeve, the colors faded, leaving it primarily dark gray.

His dark hair was thinner and streaked with gray, and his skin looked like an age-worn leather jacket that had seen better days.

"What did you do with your Harley?" She wasn't sure where that question came from, but it suddenly occurred to her she didn't know. Her dad had bought the beloved motorcycle before she was born—a 1980s sportster—and practically rebuilt the entire thing. He called it his tinkering toy, and one of her most vivid childhood memories was getting off the bus after elementary school and running to the garage to tell her dad about her day as he worked on the motorcycle.

Dad looked at her, as surprised by the question as she was. "I..." He swallowed heavily, and it occurred to her he didn't want to tell her.

Resentment bubbled up. Knowing him, he'd probably gotten drunk and driven it into a tree. "Forget it," she said, the usual hostility creeping back into her voice.

"I pushed it off Fraser Bridge."

She froze. Shocked. "What?"

"When we found out Johnnie was paralyzed from the neck down, that he'd never walk again, I drove it to Fraser Bridge and...I pushed it off."

"It's at the bottom of the lake?"

He nodded. "Yeah."

"Oh." Harley struggled to imagine how much grief and guilt her father had been suffering to do such a thing.

"Harley, I know I don't deserve your forgiveness. I've been the world's shittiest dad. But I just wanted to say I'm sorry. For all of it."

Harley's throat closed completely as she fought not to cry. It took her a few moments before she could choke out just one word. "Okay."

He didn't look at her as he spoke. Instead he leaned forward, elbows on his thighs as he ran his hands over his weary face. "I couldn't see beyond my own guilt. My own anger. I hated myself for what happened, what I'd done, so I figured everyone else must hate me too."

"I've never hated you," she whispered without hesitation. She hadn't. Despite years of anger and disappointment, she'd never once stopped loving her dad.

He glanced over his shoulder at her with a sad smile. "That's what Johnnie said too."

"When?"

"I went to see him in the hospital. Just before he..." Her dad wasn't any better at saying the words than she was. She couldn't ever seem to push out that fucking horrible word either.

This time, it needed to be said. "Died," she forced herself to finish for him.

He nodded. "Tyson came to see me. Told me Johnnie had pneumonia. That there was a good chance he wouldn't survive. He poured coffee in me until I sobered up and then Caleb drove me to the hospital and got you out of the room, so I could sneak in to see him."

Harley stared at him in quiet disbelief.

"Don't be mad at them," Dad added quickly. "I swore them to secrecy. Made them promise they wouldn't tell you I'd gone. You were devastated enough. I knew...well...I knew if you'd found out I was there, it would've just added to your pain."

Harley didn't know how to reply. So she remained quiet as her father continued speaking. "That visit, God, Harley, it changed my life. It *saved* my life."

Hearing that, she realized she wasn't angry with Tyson or Caleb. If anything, she'd just fallen even more deeply in love with her best friends. "I'm not mad."

"I told Johnnie I was sorry. Sorry for putting him in that chair." Dad ran his fingers over his mouth, his eyes unfocused, as if he was reliving that conversation. "Johnnie said he never blamed me. Not once. Said the only person in that room who couldn't forgive me for the accident was me."

Harley wiped away the tears that wouldn't be stemmed. "That sounds like Johnnie."

"Then he looked at me. Made me promise I'd look after you when he was gone."

Harley laughed though the sound came out as a choked sob. Her whole life she'd always thought she was taking care of Johnnie. It was funny to learn that he saw it the other way around.

Hell, when she considered it, he was right.

She closed her eyes and tried to pull herself together.

Her father was quiet for a few minutes, the two of them sitting side by side, both trying to battle the heavy emotions.

Finally, he said, "You know your mom's been staying at the farm, sleeping in your old room."

"Yeah," Harley said. "I know."

"You okay with that?"

Why did everyone keep asking her that question? Tyson and Caleb had asked the same thing. "Why wouldn't I be?"

Dad shrugged. "We left you alone, Harley. Made you do all the hard stuff by yourself. We deserted you and Johnnie when you needed us most."

"Granddad was there." And so many others. The Sparks' family was amazing to her and Granddad, as were Caleb's parents. They raised funds to help pay the medical bills, Chas' Uncle Julian and his construction crew donated one whole weekend to building handicapped ramps around the farm and redesigning the downstairs bathroom to accommodate Johnnie's needs. When Tyson returned from med school, he took over as Johnnie's primary physician, stopping by once, sometimes twice a week to check how her brother was doing.

When she considered it, she'd never felt alone or weighed down with responsibility. She knew there were some—maybe even Tyson and Caleb—who thought she'd taken on too much, but in her mind, the entire town had stepped up to care for her brother when her parents fell apart.

"I'm sitting on twenty years of regrets, Harley. Your mom is too. And the worst part is we have no way of fixing any of it."

She considered that. "That's not true."

Dad looked at her. "What do you mean?"

"Just stop thinking about the past and all the mistakes you've made. Stop saying it's too late. Make today day one. Start over from here. Johnnie forgave you. Granddad has taken you back into the house and put you to work on the farm. And you're talking to Mom again."

"And you?"

Harley sucked in a deep breath. Anger was nothing but an emotional drain. So was worry. She didn't have time for any of it anymore.

"I forgive you too. For all of it."

It looked as if she'd pierced a tiny hole in the balloon. One second her father was sitting next to her stiffer than a corpse. The next all the air went out, his shoulders slumped, his head bowed, and he cried.

She'd never seen her father cry. Not once.

Harley reached out, wrapping her arm around his shoulders as he quietly sobbed, his body trembling. "It's okay, Dad. It's all going to be okay."

"I miss him."

She gripped him tighter. How many times had she heard or spoken those very same words since her return? "We all do."

They sat there, huddled together for a very long time, without speaking. Once her father's tears dried, they clasped hands and watched the world go by.

Two squirrels scampered amidst the leaves, chasing each other around the thick trunk of an oak tree. A couple of birds —robins—landed nearby, pecking at something on the path. Occasionally, a jogger would pass. At least three of the runners had done a double take when they'd caught sight of Harley and her dad together. They both just smiled and waved, and then grinned conspiratorially at each other, enjoying the shock value they were provoking.

"You happy staying at Tyson's place?"

She nodded.

"Because you could come back to the farm. If it was my

presence there that made you feel like you needed to leave, we—"

"It wasn't you." She didn't move out to escape her dad. "It was time, Dad. Let's face it; I'm too old to live with my parents."

He grinned. "We all haven't lived together under the same roof in decades. I guess I thought it might be nice to try it again."

She'd taken several steps forward since coming back to Maris. Though she appreciated that her dad wanted to be close to her again, moving home would be a definite step back.

"I'm going to stay put. I really like living with Caleb and Ty."

"I'm glad you've got those boys in your life. Glad they were there to help you when I..."

"It's day one, remember?"

He rubbed his face. It was obviously going to take him time and practice to stop hating himself for all that happened. "Yeah."

Harley considered telling him that she was more than friends with Tyson and Caleb. She really didn't have a clue how anyone would take the news. She felt like she needed a gauge, someone not Art, to talk to about it.

"I love Ty and Cal." Well, that hadn't come out exactly the way she'd intended.

Dad nodded. "They're good guys."

She took a deep breath. "No. What I mean is..." She swallowed heavily, instantly regretting what she'd started. "I'm *in* love with them."

Her dad looked at her curiously, studying her face. "Do they know?"

She bit her lip as she nodded slowly. "Yeah."

"And how do they feel about that?"

"They're in love with me too."

He turned to look back out at the trees, letting the silence linger. She didn't try to explain or go into more detail. It had been hard enough to say the little bit she had. Besides, there was no way on God's green earth she was going to tell him things had progressed from friends to love to a physical affair.

She and her dad might have spent the last twenty years estranged, but now that he was sober, now that they were talking again, she recalled all too clearly the overprotective father who liked to tease her in middle school about how he intended to meet her future boyfriends. The basic plan included him sitting in the living room with his rifle over his lap. He always laughed as she protested and swore she'd never bring any boys home if he embarrassed her like that, but deep inside, she liked knowing that her daddy would do anything to keep her safe.

After far too many quiet minutes, he turned to look at her again. "You're happy?"

"Yes," she whispered. "Happier than I've ever been in my life."

He smiled. "A man can't ask for more than that for his daughter. But you know, you haven't exactly picked an easy path."

"I know. Actually, it's all really new. We plan to take our time revealing it. There are a lot of people we need to talk to first. I started with you, so thanks for being so cool and not freaking out."

"No one knows but me?"

"No."

It was as if thirty years fell away from her father's face. He sat up straighter, his shoulders no longer slumped. "You trust me?"

She did. Maybe she was a fool. After all, her dad had let her down more times than she could count in the past. But something told her this time was different. *He* was different.

He was her dad again. The one who hung the moon.

"Yes."

"I love you, Harley. I always have. I know it seems like that's not true, but...I'm not going to let you down again. If those boys are what you want, if they make you happy, you have my support."

He opened his arms and she went to him without hesitation, accepting the hug. She'd woken up this morning, snuggled between Caleb and Tyson, thinking life couldn't get much better.

She'd been wrong.

CHAPTER NINE

Tyson sat at the counter to wait for Harley and Caleb for their lunch date. He'd arrived early, so he grabbed a cup of coffee. Nighttime was always heaven. Morning was always hell. The reality of what they'd started was much clearer in broad daylight.

They were two weeks into their unconventional affair. Every sexual encounter was more explosive than the previous and in the darkest hours of night, as he lay in bed with them, he could almost believe what they had was perfect.

Almost.

Then, he woke up and all the doubts and concerns crept back in.

He was in love with Harley. Caleb was too. And neither of them minded sharing the love of their lives. Those facts remained the same.

But another thing that hadn't been a question when they'd embarked on this love affair was starting to make itself known.

Something he hadn't anticipated, hadn't considered or

even thought was a possibility. Something he hadn't let himself think, even in the depths and privacy of his own mind.

Last night, when they'd been together, touching, kissing, undressing each other, Caleb's hand had brushed Tyson's dick. And he'd felt it stir.

No. It was more than a stir. More than a simple physical response to an accidental touch. Tyson had wanted Caleb's hand on him. Wanted…

Tyson pushed the idea away. His mind was playing tricks on him. He was neck-deep in the excitement, the novelty, the newness of what he was experiencing with Harley and Caleb. That didn't mean he wanted to have sex with Caleb.

He was reading too much into it. Creating something from nothing.

Probably.

The problem was, when he'd woken up today, that new unease had been piled on top of the never-ending anxiety that came whenever he considered sitting down and talking to his parents about his new relationship.

No matter how amazing things were between the three of them in bed, it didn't mean that life was going to be all sunshine and roses. There were still too many unknowns.

Too many people to tell, to possibly lose in their lives.

Too many feelings to sort through.

Staring down at the black brew, he sighed heavily.

Macie approached him from the other side of the bar. "That's a sad sound. What's the matter, Ty? You look like you just lost your best friend."

Harley had told her dad about them earlier in the week. God. Brave woman tackled the sensitive subject immediately and Tyson envied her. She didn't have to wonder how her dad would take the news, wasn't losing sleep over the confrontation. She'd told them all about her conversation with her father in the park, his regrets and apology, her forgiveness, and then his apparent acceptance of their relationship.

Tyson hadn't seen her dad since she'd made the revelation and while she assured him her dad was cool with it, he wouldn't rest easy until he felt that truth for himself. Back in the day, her dad had been a serious badass, sporting leathers, riding the Harley around town, and cursing like a sailor. He and Caleb had thought Mr. Mills—the polar opposite of their suit-and-tie dads—was the coolest father in town, even if they were slightly terrified of him. That man had disappeared for a long time, but Tyson noticed him reemerging lately, muscles replacing the fat, the vacant expression giving way to sterner, sharper, more astute eyes.

And while Tyson had been shocked that she would confide in her dad after so many years spent estranged, Caleb was more concerned that word would get out about them before he'd had a chance to talk to his parents.

There was no denying Harley's dad had accepted the news better than Tyson and Caleb's were going to, and that didn't make it any easier to say the words.

Two weeks in, and the silence was already starting to chafe. Secrets had never come easy for Tyson. His family called him an open book, claimed that was what made him a good doctor. People could trust him to tell them the truth.

Honesty and compassion.

Those were the words his dad used to describe his bedside manner. He was proud of that description. Hiding something like this from the people he cared about didn't come easy to him, but telling them the truth wasn't simple either.

Like Caleb, he loved his family more than life itself. He looked up to his dad, thought his mom walked on water and his cousins were some of his closest friends.

Macie waved her hand in his face. "Hello. Earth to Tyson. What the hell is wrong with you?"

"I slept with Harley." The sentence ended too soon, the rest of it getting stuck in his throat.

Tyson forced himself to look at his cousin, to read her face. Caleb would read him the riot act for telling her first because…well, Macie had a well-earned reputation as a huge gossip. But he knew Macie wouldn't judge them harshly, wouldn't disapprove. She had an unconventional, wholly accepting view of the world. She was going to be the easiest person in his family to tell. Her and Jeannette.

After that, it would get tougher. Not because his other cousins would disapprove. Simply because he was fairly alpha. And until last night, he'd thought himself completely hetero. Now…

Fuck. He didn't know what he was. He was a guy sleeping with a woman with another guy in the bed. A guy whose touch…

Tyson shoved the worry away once more. He had enough on his plate just telling his family that he and Caleb were sharing Harley.

He didn't have a clue what Evan would think. Or Chas. Or Luc and Diego, for that matter. No doubt they would assume that he and Caleb were lovers as well, like they were.

Yeah. It was going to get trickier to explain to the people

who were bound to have lots of questions. Macie wasn't one of those. She'd roll with it. Like she did everything in life.

She was grinning from ear to ear. "Well, that's an interesting development."

There wasn't anyone else at the counter and his Uncle TJ, with the radar-like hearing, was next door at the bakery. The regular lunch crowd hadn't rolled in yet, so the place was relatively empty, which was why he felt safe talking to her.

"Actually, about time, I'd say."

"About time?" Tyson was surprised by the comment.

"Anyone who grew up with y'all knew there was something special there."

"Yeah," Tyson said, aware he was leaving out a big part of the story.

And because she was astute as hell, Macie knew it too. "What's Caleb think?"

He hesitated a second too long.

Macie's eyes narrowed, then her grin grew even larger. "Finish the story, Ty."

Tyson shook his head as he chuckled. "Why? You already filled in the blanks."

"Here's the thing, cuz. I don't always fill blanks in the right way. My multiple-choice answers lean toward the kinky side. Plus, Luc, Diego and Jeannette were in here this morning for breakfast, so I've got threesomes on the brain."

Tyson didn't correct her. She had it right.

"Welllll," she drawled. "How about that?"

Then she shrugged and refilled his coffee cup as if Tyson had told her nothing more exciting than there was a thirty-percent chance of rain today.

"That's all you're going to say?"

"Like I said, you three have been inseparable since the cradle practically. Don't think this announcement will shake the town off its foundation."

Only Macie would believe that.

Tyson rolled his eyes, surprised she was able to take the news in stride. Even though he'd told her because he knew she wouldn't be overly shocked, he'd expected at least some sort of amazed response. Jeez. She was acting almost bored. "The three of us are friends, Mace. We went all through school together and we have a band. I can't believe there's anything in that history that says 'these three are going to embark on a wild ménage together'."

Macie's eyes widened. "Wild, huh? Damn, I'm going to need more details. Now's a good time for me. How about you?"

Tyson laughed. God, she was good for the soul. "I wish there were more people in the world like you."

She looked horrified. "Whoa. Don't get carried away. You might want to think about that wish a little harder."

"Good point," he teased.

"So it's working out? It's okay?"

He nodded. "It's amazing."

"I'm glad Harley came home. I was worried about you guys. Never seen such sad sacks. But if it's as amazing as you say, then why the heavy sighs and gloomy look? What's wrong?"

"Caleb is worried about," he paused, then, for lack of a better description, said, "coming out."

"Coming out?"

He raised his hand quickly and shook his head. Wrong words. He wasn't even ready to admit that to himself yet. No way he'd go there with Macie. "No, no. He and I, we're not, we don't—"

"I got it, Ty. You and Caleb aren't playing hide the salami with each other. Just with Harley."

"Nice description," Tyson muttered with amused sarcasm.

"Why wouldn't you tell people about this? It's not like you're breaking new ground. Luc and Diego already did that for you, with Jeannette."

"For one thing, Cal and I are…we're *from* here. I think maybe there's a different set of expectations for us than Luc and Diego." He blew out an exasperated breath. He was doing a terrible job explaining all of this.

"Yeah. I can see where you're coming from. There are plenty of people who will think you're freaks, who'll act all disapproving, give you dirty looks, talk about you behind your backs. But so what?"

He glanced up and snorted. "So what? Seriously?"

"You and Caleb are following in your dads' footsteps. Taking on leadership roles in Maris. Even as young as you are, you've earned the respect and admiration of a lot of people around here."

"People who are going to look at us differently after this."

Macie nodded. "Yep. And some will judge you harshly. But I'm betting a lot of them won't. Because they know you, know the kind of men you are deep down. You're the good guys. There are a lot of folks in this town who really won't give a shit who you're sleeping with. And I don't think you'll miss the ones who *do* care."

"I'm a doctor, Mace. And Caleb's a businessman. I'm not sure we can snub our noses at social convention as easily as that and not suffer some repercussions."

"Like what? You'll lose patients? Caleb loses business?"

He nodded.

"Is what you have with Harley and Caleb worth that? There's another doctor in town, Ty. It's not like the people who are too appalled to be in your presence won't have medical care. And I'm damn sure you won't lose so many patients that you can't keep your practice running. God, this could actually be a good thing for you, because you're way overworked now as it is. As for Caleb's businesses, I think history has proven that most people will go for ease over principle every time. Sure, there are a handful who will boycott a fast food chain or a store if they don't agree with the owner's stance on this issue or that, but there are just as many who will keep buying stuff there because they don't want to drive twenty minutes away to the next closest store. Caleb will be fine."

"What about my dad and Cal's?"

"Ah. And now we get to the heart of the matter. It's not the town you're worried about."

"I always imagined this part of my life would be easy. I'd meet a girl, fall in love, take her home to meet my parents. Proposal, marriage, kids, happy life."

"That's not happening now?"

Tyson was quick to correct her misunderstanding. "Oh no. That's all happening. I've never been in a relationship that felt this good. All the pieces just fell together. But…"

"But there's another guy there with the same plans, same girl. How is that going to work?"

Tyson didn't have a clue. Harley mentioned last night that they should probably start figuring out answers to the hard questions. The ones people were going to ask.

Caleb insisted it was still too soon to worry about stuff like marriage and kids. And Tyson found it hard to argue. It probably *was* too soon.

Then he decided it wasn't.

They'd been friends forever, so it didn't feel like they were jumping into this relationship at the beginning. Rather, for Tyson, it was almost as if they'd been a trio for much longer. For him, it had really started just over a year ago when they'd kissed in the barn. From that day on, he'd begun to view them as his, and he'd known he would never want anyone else in his life.

"I don't know how any of it's going to work," he admitted.

"Want some advice?"

He chuckled. "Would you hold back if I said no?"

She shook her head. "Absolutely not. Figure out the answers to all the questions before you go talk to Uncle George and Mr. Hott. Because I promise you they're going to come at you with lots of them. Be prepared."

It was good advice. He was going to start the conversation Harley had begun last night. And this time they were going to finish it. "Okay."

"And if you think it would help with the rest—your worries about how the town will accept you—you guys could also talk to Amanda. She faced something similar to this when she came back home to Maris with a girlfriend in tow."

Amanda was one of Macie's best friends. And Macie was right. It had been a bit of a shake-up when Amanda returned from college with Brandi. But the hubbub died down eventually and now the two women were planning their wedding. With Macie as the officiant. The family was having a lot of fun imagining Macie presiding over anyone's marriage, but Tyson suspected she'd do a great job.

"That's probably not a bad idea. I was going to talk to Jeannette, Luc and Diego too."

"See? Lots of people. Lots of ways to fall in love. And they're all still here in Maris, living normal lives. They weren't run out of town on a rail. You guys won't be either."

Macie's response to his news, as well as her insight into human nature, had helped set his mind at ease. "Thanks, Mace. Seriously. Talking to you—"

She waved him off, interrupting before he could finish. "I'm a bartender, Ty. And brilliant, to boot. You came to the right place."

He grasped her hand, appreciating her humor. He gave it a squeeze. "I know you were joking, but you really *are* brilliant."

She flushed slightly, clearly delighted by his compliment. And then, because she had the attention span of a flea, she changed the subject. "Y'all ready to play at Sydney's wedding? Only two more weeks to go."

"We're ready."

"It's going to be the party of the century," Macie declared. There was nothing his cousin liked more than a good party.

Tyson nodded. "It's going to be great." They continued to chat about the upcoming nuptials for a bit.

Then Coop walked in and claimed what Tyson had noticed seemed to be the man's usual spot at the bar. As always, Coop smiled at Macie, and Tyson couldn't help but wonder, as he always did, if the widower wasn't carrying a torch for his cousin. Not that Tyson would mind that. Hank Cooper was a good guy, right to the core. Tyson had been his wife Sharon's primary care physician, and he'd had a lot of time to get to know the man as Sharon battled, then lost her life to cancer. Coop had been by her side the entire time, caring for her, completely devoted and wonderful.

While he couldn't help but think Macie would be lucky to date Coop, Tyson also felt very strongly that Coop would be pretty damn fortunate too. Macie was a live wire with an abundance of energy and a bit of a crazy streak, but she was going to make some man's life a hell of a lot of fun one day.

"What's new?" Coop asked.

Macie looked at Tyson as she spoke. "Tyson's involved in a scandalous affair at the moment and I'm pea-green with envy."

Tyson closed his eyes and reconsidered every nice thought he'd had about his cousin.

"Is that right?" Coop asked, looking over at Tyson. "Good for you."

And just like that, the conversation ended as Macie winked at Tyson. While Coop studied the menu, she mouthed the words, "I won't tell anyone" to Ty. He smiled and knew she wouldn't. She'd take the secret to the grave if need be—but she'd also be ready to rub it in TJ's face that she knew first, as well.

"Come on, Coop. Stop screwing around with the menu. We both know you're going to order the special."

Coop chuckled as he handed her the menu back. "Give me the special."

Macie started chatting with Coop about Sydney's wedding and her plans for Amanda's ceremony. Coop did a lot of nodding, while murmuring the occasional "yes" or "mmmh-mm," but other than that, Macie carried the conversation.

Caleb and Harley entered the restaurant together, so

Tyson grabbed his coffee cup to join them at a booth near the wall. "I'll catch you guys later."

It was Friday and they'd decided to make it a half day. Tyson was off work from now until Monday morning. And he intended to spend at least ninety-five percent of that time naked and in bed with them.

He claimed the spot next to Harley in the booth and set his cup down. "I told Macie about the three of us."

Caleb winced. "You did *what?*"

Tyson tried to fight back the anger he felt at Caleb's offended tone. "I told her."

"Jesus, Ty, why don't you just hang the news up on a billboard on the highway? I suspect it would reach about the same number of people."

Tyson scowled at his friend. "Macie won't tell."

Caleb rolled his eyes and looked away, making it clear he didn't agree with that reassurance.

"What did she say?" Harley asked.

Tyson grinned despite his annoyance with Caleb. "It's Macie."

He let that answer his question and Harley laughed. "Cool. Score one more for our side."

"It's not a contest," Caleb muttered. "And it's hardly fair when you consider who you've told. You started with the gimmes." It was clear the stress of talking to his father was starting to get to Caleb. Tyson realized his friend wasn't upset that he'd told Macie. It was more like he was upset with *himself* for not being able to do the same.

"I know it's only been a couple of weeks," Harley said as she grasped Caleb's hand and gave it a gentle squeeze. "Feels like longer though, doesn't it?"

Tyson nodded. "I've loved you since we were kids, and I fell in love with you that day in the barn last year when we kissed."

"Change of plans," Caleb said, rising from the booth. "Come on."

Tyson stood as well, confused, and then Harley followed him out of the booth. "Where are we going?"

"You'll see."

Caleb bypassed their cars in the parking lot and the three of them walked a touch too quickly and in silence for several blocks, until Tyson figured out where they were headed.

They walked toward the gazebo that sat in the center of the park. It was a pretty day, so there were a few people out, taking advantage of the sunshine, eating picnic lunches, tossing Frisbees and playing with their dogs.

They climbed the steps to the empty gazebo and together they turned to look out at the large, open grassy area before them.

"I fell in love with you two right here," Caleb said. "Our first public gig, remember? Tyson's dad told us it was time we stopped messing around in the basement. He got us the gig and we played a handful of songs at the Maris Barbeque Festival. That field out there was packed with people and we were all standing up here—nervous, excited, terrified."

Tyson could see everything Caleb described, recalled the day as if it were yesterday.

"It was our senior year," Harley added as she pointed to the left. "Johnnie sat right over there under that tree with Granddad. They were so proud of me that day."

Caleb rested his hands on the railing. "Everyone was. Not many people had heard us play before that and I don't think their expectations were too high. Think they thought we'd bang out a few clangers, they'd clap politely, and that would be it."

"We rocked it," Tyson said, remembering his cousins jumping up and down and screaming out his name after every song. The way his dad gave him a thumbs-up at the end of the performance. He'd never questioned his father's love, but just the same, whenever Tyson could gain his approval—something that required quite a bit of work—he remembered it, savored it.

Caleb nodded. "We put it all out there, played our hearts out, showed them what we were capable of. The whole town looked at us differently that day. Suddenly we weren't just a bunch of rowdy teenagers. We had something that set us apart, that made us special."

Tyson felt uneasy. "Why are we here, Cal?"

"Look around."

Tyson followed Caleb's gaze around the park. There wasn't anyone there who he didn't know by name. Hell, he could have named their parents, siblings, jobs, and told at least one funny story about over half the folks there.

"We have to put it all out there one more time. Show them our hearts. And believe me, this time, they will see us differently again."

Something Macie had said earlier stuck with him, so Tyson repeated it. "Is the regard of this town more important than what we have?"

Harley's eyes were glued to Caleb's face, and Tyson could see the anxiety she was feeling.

Caleb never hesitated. He shook his head. "No. It's not. But I love this town too. Love the people in it. My parents aren't like y'alls. They won't get this. They won't. And I have to figure out a way to tell them, to make them understand it. I just need a little bit more time."

Tyson felt guilty for pushing the issue. He should have known this would be harder for Caleb. He wasn't the type to throw caution to the wind. He took calculated risks and when it came to people he cared about, people he loved, he would work overtime to ensure he never hurt them.

"Or," Harley said with a twinkle in her eye. "We could just strip off all our clothes and go at it like sex maniacs, right here on the gazebo, right now."

Tyson chuckled and Caleb grinned as he shook his head. "You're twisted, Harley. You're getting to be as bad as Macie, seeing everything from some weird perspective."

Tyson expected her to continue the joke, so he was surprised when her face sobered.

"Actually, I think I'm the only one looking at this from the *right* perspective. Johnnie died when he was only twenty-nine years old. He never got married, had kids, bought a house. He never got to dance to the 'Orange Blossom Special' with his own legs. Despite all that, he was one of the happiest people I've ever known.

"We are so blessed. We have our health and the chance to live out something truly amazing. And yeah, Cal, maybe people will judge us for it. But I don't care. Johnnie faced some of the most horrific limits I can imagine—not being able to walk, to feed himself, to move his arms. And he still retained his humor, his love of life. He found ways to dance at the barn parties; he was all over that damn farm, telling me how to do everything. He was a voracious reader, he loved music and art, and he laughed all the time. Plus, he never missed his weekly lunch date at the restaurant with Macie. What if someone had looked at him and said, 'You shouldn't do any of that because people in wheelchairs should stay home where we don't have to see them'? What if he'd let someone else limit what he wanted to do?"

Tyson was blown away by her elegance, by her conviction, by her strength. "I would have liked to see someone try to hold Johnnie back. He'd have run the asshole over with his chair."

"Then backed up and done it again," Caleb added. "Harley—"

"You're letting other people set the limits. It's your life, Cal. Your future, your happiness. Just answer one question for me. Do you want *more*?"

Caleb didn't hesitate. He nodded. "You know I do."

"How much more?"

Tyson wasn't sure what to think when Caleb's gaze traveled to him. "All of it. I want all of it."

"Come on," Harley said, taking Caleb's hand. They walked in silence as they returned to the restaurant.

"Where to?"

She tugged him toward her car. "You're not the only person with a special place. Can you guys leave your cars here this weekend?"

There were plenty of spots in the Sparks Barbeque parking lot. Tyson nodded. "Yeah. I'm sure they'll be fine. Why?"

"You'll see."

They drove out of town and headed for her family's farm. Tyson knew this route as well as the back of his hand. "The farm?"

Harley grinned as she pulled down the driveway that led to the farmhouse. "Not exactly. I came out earlier today and set up a few things with Granddad's help."

"Did you tell him too?" Caleb asked.

Harley shook her head. "No. Not yet. You're not the only one struggling to come clean, Cal. I mean, Granddad is super cool, but there's a definite awkward factor when you consider I have to tell my seventy-five-year-old grandfather I'm shacking up with two guys. I'm pretty sure I'll die of embarrassment before I get the words out."

Tyson chuckled. "Just make sure we're nowhere near when you break the news."

"Chicken shit," she taunted with a grin.

She parked her car by the barn, not bothering to go into the house. As they entered the building, Tyson spotted the three horses, all saddled with familiar packs on their backs.

"Camping?" he asked, though it was obvious that was her intention. The three of them—sometimes with Logan, sometimes without—had gone on more weekend camping excursions than he could count.

"Yep. Thought we were due for a trip."

"I love it," Caleb said, hugging Harley. "And I love you."

"We're all thinking too hard lately. The only time things feel completely right are when we're alone together. So let's go be alone, fuck each other's brains out, and then come back stronger."

"Let me get this straight," Caleb said. "You're seducing us in hopes of distracting us and making us forget what we were just talking about?"

Harley gave Caleb a sheepish grin. "Um. Yeah?"

His eyes were serious when he nodded slowly. "I have absolutely no problem with that."

"Everything we need in those packs?" Tyson asked.

"Yep."

"Then let's go."

CHAPTER TEN

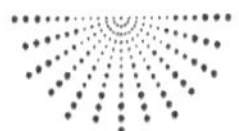

Harley finished gathering kindling for the fire pit as Tyson and Caleb put up the tent. In the past, whenever they went camping, they'd brought two tents. One for the guys and one for her. This time, they just brought a four-man one.

"Good thing you remembered the tent stakes, Harley," Tyson joked as Caleb flipped him the bird.

Harley laughed. "I'm more responsible than Cal."

Caleb shot them both dirty looks. "One time. It was only one time I forgot the damn things. And it wasn't like we had to rough it. We just had to pile into one tent."

"A two-man tent," Harley reminded him. They had teased Caleb about the misadventures of that camping trip for years. It had been the summer after the guys' freshman year in college. They were home for the summer and Caleb declared one morning that they were going camping. Harley had been in Dallas with Johnnie for a doctor's appointment and Logan and Tyson were both working, so Caleb assured them he'd take care of packing everything they needed, so as soon as they arrived at the farm they could head out to the campsite. Otherwise, they'd be traveling through the woods and arriving after dark—which was the reason *all* of them had given Caleb for waiting until the next day, when they had more time to prepare. However, he had it in his head they needed to go sooner rather than later, so they entrusted him to do all the preparations.

Tyson staked down one corner of the tent. "We were stacked up like sardines in that thing. Pretty sure I didn't get five minutes of sleep. Woke up with Logan's elbow pressing against my face and Harley's knee in my back."

"It wouldn't have been a big deal if it hadn't started raining. A couple of us could have stayed outside otherwise." Caleb used that defense every time.

And now, like always, they ignored it.

Harley snapped a branch in half, adding it to the pit. "Between the storm and being squished half to death in the middle of you guys, it was a long damn night."

The second she mentioned her placement in the tent, she felt two pairs of eyes on her. No doubt they were recalling that night as well. Logan had been on one end, Caleb on the other. She and Tyson were jammed into the center, and that was the first time she'd slept between her two guys.

She had always lied about her reasons for not being able to sleep. In truth, she'd felt a sexual attraction, a pull to them. She hadn't acted on it, but she had lain there all night, imagining things she thought could never come to pass.

The last couple of weeks had proven her wrong on that count.

"I had a hard-on that whole night," Caleb confessed.

Tyson snorted. "You get hard when there's a strong wind or whenever you smell bacon. That's hardly news."

Caleb chucked a small stone at his friend, but Tyson deftly dodged it.

"Maybe so, Ty, but when I think about it, that night was the first time I wondered…"

Harley agreed with Caleb's statement. "I wondered too, Cal."

Tyson swallowed heavily. "Yeah. So did I. Of course, we were all twenty, which when you think about it is synonymous with horny. And while this works as a threesome, Logan was there too, and he would *not* make for a happy foursome. Son of a bitch snores something awful."

Harley dropped down on one of the logs set up by the pit as a seat. Her granddad had built this campsite at the edge of their farm nearly fifty years earlier. He'd brought her dad out here when he was younger, and then her and Johnnie, back before the accident. It was an eight-mile ride by horseback and it sat next to the river. They were surrounded by nothing but woods. It was peaceful, picturesque, perfect.

It was Harley's retreat. Sometimes she'd simply ride out here for the day when she needed to get away. She'd arrive in the morning, cook lunch over the fire pit, sit by the river with her feet in the water, and then she'd ride back in the afternoon. She'd come here the day after Johnnie died, sobbing out her sorrow to the trees and the water.

She was glad to be here again, happy to be here with Caleb and Tyson. This place always seemed to soak into her skin, clean out all the dust and grime life left there, and made her stronger. "I wonder how things would be now if we'd given in all those years ago."

Caleb claimed the log next to her. "Probably would have been a mistake back then. The timing was wrong. None of us were in the right place for something permanent. Besides, we were all still young and stupid. We'd have found a way to fuck it up."

"I'm glad we didn't give in," Tyson said, as he bent down to start the fire. "It might have messed up the friendship. Might have caused us to all go our separate ways."

"Funny how one decision made a dozen years ago could have such a huge impact on the present, isn't it?" Harley wasn't just thinking of the camping trip, but of Johnnie pleading to get on the back of their dad's motorcycle as well.

"Let's have some dinner," Caleb said, when it was obvious her thoughts had drifted down a darker path.

Happy for something to distract her, Harley pulled out the fixings for mountain pies, handing Caleb one of the irons. Once the fire was hot enough, they cooked their pizza pockets in the cast iron pans and passed around a bottle of Crown Royal.

The guys grinned when she revealed the ukulele she'd stashed in one of the packs. As she strummed, they sang together. She started with her favorite, "Somewhere Over the Rainbow," then she taught them an Ingrid Michaelson one she'd learned in Florida, called, "You and I." They laughed at the lyrics and decided to add it to their set to play at the next barn dance.

Hours had passed since the sunset, but none of them moved. While the sexual pull was there, and growing more intense by the minute, they didn't rush it. Instead they let it build, throwing more fuel on it with heated looks and the slow shedding of clothing.

It was a warm night. Though the sun was long gone, the humidity and heat of the day hadn't abated at all. They discussed skinny-dipping in the river to cool off, but decided they were too lazy, too comfortable where they were to move.

Harley had declared, the last time they dove into the lake naked as the day they were born, that she was never wasting money on another swimsuit as long as she lived. There was something so ridiculously freeing about floating in the water without clothing on. Caleb and Tyson joked about creating a monster, but neither of them had disagreed.

"This was the perfect day, angel," Caleb said, scooting closer to her, so he could drape his arm over her shoulder. "Thanks for thinking of it."

She rested her head on the crook of his shoulder and closed her eyes for a little while. His shirt had soaked up the smell of the campfire and she breathed it in deeply. She loved that scent—wood and fire and outdoors.

One second they were sitting there, peaceful, relaxed—the next, the sparks began to fly. She wasn't sure who moved first.

Harley lifted her head from Caleb's shoulder as his hand cupped her cheek. After the carefree easiness of their day, she expected a slow, gentle kiss. What she got was fireworks.

Caleb kissed her like he'd never touched her lips before. His were hard, demanding, so hungry. She opened her mouth and his tongue was there, exploring. No, it was more like plundering, taking her mouth captive with no demand for ransom. His hands were firm on her face, tilting her head whenever he wanted deeper access.

Harley struggled to breathe, but Caleb didn't seem concerned about her need for air.

Tyson only added to the intensity of the moment. While

she was overwhelmed by Caleb's powerful kiss, that didn't mean she wasn't acutely aware of what Tyson was doing.

He'd taken his position on the other side of her. As Caleb twisted her to face him more fully, Tyson wrapped his arms around her waist from behind, sliding his hands under her shirt. He roughly tugged her bra beneath her breasts so that he could palm her flesh, then lightly pinch her tight nipples.

She moaned, the sound captured by Caleb's mouth, when Tyson nipped the side of her neck, then licked the pain away.

Harley wasn't certain what had changed, but the kid gloves had come off tonight. The past two weeks, their lovemaking had been just that—making love. Softer touches and kisses. They'd played the role of gentle lovers, giving the lion's share of control to her. She suspected they'd done so in order to make sure she felt safe, secure. The three of them would undress, crawl into bed, and then he and Caleb would take turns making love to her. It was hot, sexy as hell, and yet, there was no denying that tonight, they wanted more.

Harley sensed something was still missing. And while she thought she knew what it was, she didn't have a clue how to approach her suspicions with the guys. She was afraid they'd freak out and she'd ruin everything.

When she thought she was going to pass out from lack of air, Harley shoved on Caleb's shoulders, forcing him to release her.

He scowled, but he gave way.

"Caleb," she gasped.

He spoke to her, but Caleb's gaze was locked on Tyson's face behind her. "Lose the shirt. And the bra."

Tyson lost no time grabbing the hem of her shirt and tugging it off. Her bra followed just as quickly.

Tyson's hands fell to the waistband of her shorts. "Actually, I think *you* should take off the rest of your clothes."

Harley didn't respond, didn't move until Caleb added, "Now, sweetheart," in a deep, demanding voice.

"God, you know what that voice does to me," she teased.

Caleb grinned. "That's why I use it. Strip, gorgeous."

The devil in her was tempted to push things as well. "What if I don't?"

Caleb's gaze darkened, not with anger, but with lust. "We've spent years talking about our desires, Harley. What we like in bed, what we like to do with our lovers. You've been there. You've heard it all. Do you think we'd want less from you?"

She remembered their stories, recalled how they'd impacted her so strongly. Made her so freaking horny, she'd gone home and masturbated, imagining Tyson and/or Caleb tying her up, pulling her over their laps to spank her, withholding her orgasm until she nearly exploded with need. They'd drawn pictures with their sex stories, and there was no denying she wanted to experience it all.

"I know what you like," she admitted.

"And?" Tyson prompted.

"It's just that…usually…my past lovers…" Her words kept coming out in starts and stops as she felt her way around what she wanted to say. "They weren't really, that, um, into me. I mean the sex was hot and stuff, but I've never really tried anything kinkier than sixty-nine."

Tyson moved slightly to her side and tugged her face to him. "We can keep the status quo, Harley. I love everything we do together in bed. It's sexy and hot. We'd never push you beyond what you're comfortable doing."

There was an unspoken "but" at the end of that sentence. They all heard it as loudly as if he'd said the word.

"But," she finished for him, "we've only scratched the surface." Harley forced herself to say more, to try to feel out how they might respond to even more than they were proposing. "In what you can do with me. And what you can do with each other."

Tyson froze, his gaze quickly darting to Caleb before looking away again.

His response and something in his face told Harley she wasn't the only one who'd sensed a slight tug between Caleb and Tyson.

Caleb blew out a long breath. And then, dove in with both feet. "A lifetime is a long time. To explore all of that and more."

Tyson's gaze returned to his friend's face and held. "Cal?"

Caleb shrugged. While they'd both revealed the interest, it seemed they weren't ready to go any further than talk. "Let's focus on the other stuff tonight, Harley."

She released a nervous breath. "Other stuff?"

He gave her a wicked grin. "We'll go slow...ish."

She laughed. "You're an asshole. But you're *my* asshole." She stood up and both men moved back to give her some space. She dropped her shorts and panties in one fluid motion.

Though the campfire was starting to fade, it still provided more than enough light for them to see her clearly. And for her to see them.

Four hungry eyes were pointed in her direction, which seemed appropriate for the setting. She was the prey and these sexy wolves were ready to pounce.

She lifted her arms. "I'm yours," she whispered.

Caleb was the first to react, but only by a split second.

Tyson moved until he was directly behind her. He reached for one wrist and then the other, pulling them together at the base of her back and holding them there. When she tried to tug one loose, he tightened his hold.

His grip forced her shoulders back, which caused her breasts to thrust out.

"You're so beautiful," Tyson murmured into her ear. His sweet words were in direct opposition to Caleb's touch. He reached out, roughly palming her breasts before pinching both nipples.

Harley jerked as if struck by lightning. Her pussy began to throb. She was completely naked, both men fully dressed.

Caleb continued to play with her breasts as Tyson held her captive for the sensual assault. Then Tyson's lips found their way to her neck. Harley tilted her head to give him better access. He took advantage of the bared skin, licking, sucking, nipping.

Harley fought briefly against Tyson's grip. She was too used to participating. She missed touching them, guiding them. He tightened the hold, and then lifted his head.

"Give me something to tie her up with, Cal."

Caleb released her breasts without comment, turning toward the tent. There were some straps she'd used to cinch up the sleeping bags. Grabbing one, he returned, spinning her toward the fire as he and Tyson remained behind her. She wasn't sure which of them tied her hands together at the base of her back, but they knew their stuff.

Her arousal rose even higher.

"This is so amazing," she muttered.

Tyson chuckled. "Jesus. You realize that's only going to encourage us."

"I don't care." She didn't.

Caleb returned to the tent, dragging out one of the sleeping bags. He folded it up several times until it was a thick cushion. Then he guided her down to her knees.

"I want your mouth on my dick," he said, his voice gruff with need.

Harley wanted that too. "Give it to me."

Caleb shoved his shorts down, kicking them off. He went commando. They both did.

He stepped closer, guiding his cock to her lips. She licked the underside in one long stroke, loving the groan her action produced.

Harley looked up at Tyson. "I want you too."

Tyson dropped his shorts, fisting his dick, stroking it with a hard grip. Neither man seemed to crave gentleness. They liked stronger, rougher touches, and they'd taught her to appreciate the same.

While she loved everything they'd done together prior to this, Harley realized that tonight—for the first time—she was going to meet her true lovers.

"Give it to me," she whispered.

Tyson pushed closer. Not content with just her tongue, he pressed the head of his cock into her mouth, not stopping until he thrust his way straight to the back of her throat.

Harley opened wider, taking as much as she could. She was starving for this, ravenous.

Tyson gripped her head, his fingers tangling in her hair as he pumped in one, two, three times. Then he stepped back to allow Caleb to take his place.

They continued to take turns, thrusting into her mouth. Harley longed to touch them, struggling against the restraints.

Caleb noticed. He dropped down to his knees in front of her as Tyson fucked her mouth. "You want free, Harl?"

She nodded, the movement causing Tyson to moan and push in deeper.

"Tough," Caleb taunted.

She narrowed her eyes, but the look only prompted a wicked chuckle.

"You're ours, remember?"

Harley didn't bother to correct him. She couldn't. Tyson wasn't giving her a chance to enter this conversation. He pressed deep inside her mouth once again.

"What would you do if you were free?" he asked, his lips hot against her cheek, the words a mere rumble near her ear.

Her eyes closed as she imagined cupping their balls, gripping the base of their dicks. Adding her own tight stroke to the work of her mouth. Driving them to completion. She loved the sounds Tyson and Caleb made when they came. The almost pained curses, the sweet nothings, the words of love that spilled from their lips as they filled her.

She loved knowing that she could provoke that passion, that desire, that need from them. They were strong, powerful men. And yet, she had the ability to bring them to their knees. It was a heady feeling she'd never tire of.

Caleb glanced up at Tyson. She wasn't sure what sort of telepathy they shared, but she'd noticed on more than one occasion, they spoke some silent language with their eyes.

Tyson tugged his cock free from her mouth.

"What would you do?" Caleb repeated the question.

She told them exactly what she'd imagined. The walls

between them had fallen fast. Words that would have prompted one hell of a blush with previous lovers fell from her lips without so much as a stutter. "I'd touch your balls. Squeeze them."

Caleb nodded—and then he shocked the hell out of her. *And* Tyson.

"Like this?" Caleb took Tyson's balls in his own hand, gripping them tightly, even as Tyson jerked at the unexpected touch.

"Jesus. Cal." Tyson's tone was breathless and it told Harley—and Caleb—exactly what they needed to know. He liked it. A lot.

Tyson made no attempt to push his friend's hand away. Apart from the brief burst of surprise, he held steady, his gaze locked on Caleb's.

Caleb's fingers moved slowly, stroking Tyson's balls. It felt like he was waiting for something.

Finally, Tyson smiled. "Yeah. Okay."

Permission.

They'd obviously known each other long enough that a lot of words weren't needed.

"A lifetime, Ty. I want a lifetime with the two of you."

Tyson nodded. "I want the same, but..."

Caleb grinned. "I don't want to fuck you, Ty. At least..." He paused and swallowed heavily. "At least, not yet. But I'm not going to keep avoiding you, either."

Harley considered their conversation, recalled their previous encounters. Both men took turns and there was no denying she'd been the barrier between them. They each claimed one side and they remained there, taking care not to breach the invisible property line.

"Can I just take one second to say," Harley let her gaze point to Caleb's hand engulfing Tyson's balls, since her hands were bound, "that is *really* fucking hot?"

"What else would you do, angel?" Caleb prompted.

Just like that, Caleb had found a way to give her control even though he'd taken it away with the strap around her wrists.

"Grip the base of his dick while I take the head in my mouth."

Tyson groaned before either of them even made a move. "You do that and this isn't going to last long."

"You want to come in her mouth or pussy?" Caleb asked.

"Both," Tyson admitted.

Caleb chuckled. "Greedy bastard."

Caleb grasped his friend's cock the way she requested and guided Tyson back to her lips as she opened them. She and Caleb worked together, driving Tyson to climax. Caleb released him mere seconds before Tyson came, moving back slightly to watch them.

Tyson gripped her hair, tugging it as he exploded. Neither man had touched her elsewhere, and Harley was aching with need. She shivered and cried out when Caleb reached down to stroke her clit.

Tyson remained in her mouth for a few moments, pulling himself together as Caleb drove Harley crazy, rubbing her clit harder, faster. Her hips tilted forward to seek out even more of the stimulation.

When Tyson withdrew from her mouth, he stepped behind her and released the ties on her arms. She started to reach out for Caleb, but Tyson kept her arms pressed to her sides.

"No. Keep them there. Spread your legs farther apart," Tyson commanded.

She did as he asked without delay and was rewarded when Tyson reached between her outstretched thighs from behind. He swept two fingers along her slit, dragging the wetness of her pussy all the way to her ass. He used it to allow him to press the tip of one finger into her anus.

They'd touched her there before and she knew what the end goal was. She'd read books, seen porn on the Internet, and her imagination wasn't that limited.

Two guys. One girl. It didn't take a genius to figure out all the ways the three of them could come together.

"Tyson," she whispered, pressing her ass back toward his finger.

"Not tonight, gorgeous."

"But—" she started.

"No." His word was strong and left no doubt he wasn't going to be swayed. "Not tonight. When we do that, we're going to have lots of lube and a bed."

"Jesus," Caleb muttered. "Y'all are going to have to talk about something else. Just the thought of that has me ready to blow."

Harley giggled, but the sound was cut short when Tyson's fingers returned to her pussy and he thrust two inside, hard and deep.

Caleb returned to his feet and pressed his cock back into Harley's mouth as Tyson fucked her with his fingers.

"Come on, love. Let's come together."

Caleb thrust into her mouth as Tyson found all the right places, every hot button that existed below her waist.

Twice she started to reach out for Caleb, only to be stopped by Tyson.

"Let me," Tyson said, giving Caleb a taste of his own medicine when he cupped his balls and squeezed.

"Fuck. Damn, man. I didn't realize that…"

"I know," Tyson confirmed.

Harley felt a bit like laughing, simply from the sheer joy of the moment. Every single time they came together was better than the last. And tonight they'd thrown open all the windows and doors, washing them all in bright, beautiful, warm sunlight.

Caleb grunted when Tyson squeezed his balls again, the touch all he needed to fall over. He came within seconds, filling Harley's mouth as she drank him down.

Once Caleb recovered, they lifted Harley from the sleeping bag and led her to the tent. Laying her on her back, Tyson bent down, licking and sucking her clit, fucking her with his tongue and fingers as Caleb laid claim to her breasts.

She came three times before they were finished. Then the three of them fell together into a heap of naked, sweaty bodies. While Harley remained in the middle, this time Caleb's hand extended beyond her, resting on Tyson's waist. And Tyson's lay on Caleb's ass.

"Love you," she murmured as sleep came to claim her quickly.

The last thing she recalled was Caleb muttering the same as Tyson kissed her bare shoulder.

Heaven. She'd found heaven.

CHAPTER ELEVEN

Tyson stood on the stage and watched as Sydney and Chas swayed around the dance floor. The newlyweds had chosen an appropriate song. Harley and Caleb joined him on the chorus of "I Don't Dance" and there were very few dry eyes in the place.

He glanced over at Harley as she strummed her guitar. She winked at him and smiled. She looked stunning tonight in a new red dress that hit mid-thigh and gave him just enough of a peek at her breasts to make his cock twitch. Her hair was pinned up with a few loose pieces curling around her cheeks. He had every intention of pulling those pins out one by one tonight, then wrapping those dark strands around his fingers and tugging on it until she moaned.

Tyson forced his eyes away from her when he missed the cue for the second verse. The four of them had played together long enough to cover up the mistake without anyone noticing except them. He started singing and caught Caleb's shit-eating grin out of the corner of his eye. No doubt his friend knew exactly what had distracted him.

It had taken every ounce of willpower they both had just to let her get in the car to come to the wedding when she'd walked out of her bedroom earlier. Tyson had let loose with a wolf-whistle, and Caleb had backed her against a wall, running his hand along her bare thigh beneath the shimmery material. They'd kissed as Tyson had watched and silently plotted their next twenty minutes. It included Harley riding Caleb as he fucked her ass from behind.

They hadn't gone there yet. They hadn't gone a *lot* of places yet. Each night they inched closer, but none of them seemed ready to pull out the big guns in their sexual arsenal. He and Caleb had stopped avoiding each other in bed, touching each other more and more. But Tyson was hesitant to push for anything else. They hadn't kissed, hadn't sucked, hadn't fucked.

It was as if they'd acknowledged the possibility of such an event, but neither of them was ready to go there yet. Jesus. Just initiating a threesome with Harley had been intimidating enough. And they hadn't yet fully explored everything *that* unique, sexy-as-fuck relationship offered.

Unfortunately, before Tyson could voice his desires back at the house, Harley—Miss Practicality—had shoved Caleb back, glanced at the clock and informed them they were already running late. Then she'd given them a rain check.

If she knew what he was hoping to claim tonight, Tyson doubted she would have thrown the promise out there so frivolously. Of course, he hadn't talked to Caleb about that desire either. Not that he thought his friend would object. Knowing that kinky bastard, he probably had the same fantasy.

Tyson grinned at the thought, then messed up a word and

shoved every image of Caleb and Harley out of his mind. Otherwise, this was going to be a very long—and stiff—reception. He tried to wiggle his hips slightly to adjust his pants without his hands. Thank God for the guitar in front of him.

Time to get himself back on track before he embarrassed himself. Looking out into the crowd, he found his parents sitting at one of the front tables, smiling at him. Phyllis Barton was at a nearby table and it appeared she'd set up her son, Eugene, with Lorraine, the new beautician at the beauty parlor. Neither Eugene nor Lorraine looked very interested in the matchup as their bored eyes wandered the room. Chas' grandmother sat with his Uncle Julian, and they both looked so proud they could pop.

Studying the crowd helped Tyson regain control.

The bride and groom smiled each other, Sydney singing along with their band as Chas held her close. The wedding had been beautiful and throughout the ceremony, he and Caleb had covertly held hands with Harley. Tyson longed for the day when they could find some way to make a similar "'til death do us part" commitment to each other. Though God only knew how that would work. Shit, they hadn't managed to break the news of their relationship to anyone other than Harley's dad and Macie yet. Not that they'd tried. Tyson had stopped worrying about what others thought the second Caleb touched his balls. Since then, he'd been struggling to understand and accept how fucking much he loved it. And how he wanted more.

Lacy sat at a table near the stage, her eyes locked on Logan as he played the bass. Though they were nowhere near the dance floor, it felt almost as if the two of them were swaying in time to the music together.

Evan held his young daughter, Eryn, in one arm, his other wrapped around his wife Annie's waist. They'd been together for years, yet they still looked at each other as if they'd fallen in love yesterday.

He was delighted for his cousins and the happiness they'd found. In the past, he'd acknowledged their relationships, but he'd never truly recognized the emotions. Probably because when he looked back, he knew the love he'd professed for his past lovers hadn't come close to touching what he felt for Harley and Caleb.

God. The wedding was working on him, making him want what the other couples on the dance floor had. A right to show how he felt. A right to stand next to Caleb and Harley and say, "This is it. They're the ones I love. The ones I want to spend the rest of my life with."

That feeling grew as he watched Jeannette at a corner table with Luc and Diego. The three of them were sitting close, not bothering to hide how they felt. Luc's fingers toyed with Jeannette's hair as his arm rested along the back of her chair. Diego held her hand and every now and then, he'd lift it for a kiss that never failed to make Jeannette smile and blush.

As the song came to an end, everyone clapped and Tyson stepped off the side of the stage with Caleb, Logan and Harley. Sydney and Chas had hired a deejay for the rest of the evening, insisting they wanted Tyson's band to be guests at the wedding, able to enjoy the night without having to play the entire time.

Logan placed his bass in its case, and then excused himself to go find Lacy. Tyson had teased his friend about the rubber band attached to him and his cousin, claiming Logan and Lacy couldn't get more than a few feet apart before the band snapped them back together. Now he knew exactly what that same tight pull felt like. It was nearly impossible to resist the draw to return to his lovers whenever he was away from them.

He'd heard about the honeymoon phase, but he'd never truly experienced it. Right now, he was knee-deep in it.

"That was great, Ty," Harley said, as she and Caleb put their instruments away. Tyson reached for her, unable to deny himself the chance to touch her. He gave her a big hug and just barely managed to refrain from kissing her.

"Thanks, love."

Caleb watched them, smiling and rolling his eyes. "Tonight's going to be tough. Nothing like a wedding to make a guy's dick hard."

Harley laughed. "Very romantic, Cal."

He shrugged. "What can I say? I've got a way with sweet words, buttercup."

Harley wrapped her arm through Caleb's. "I thought it was just women who were overly sensitive to weddings and all they represent."

"You realize neither one of you is talking about the same thing, right?" Tyson asked. "Cal looks around this room, sees all the dancing couples, and thinks sex. You're looking around, Harl, and seeing rings, flowers, future babies and forever."

Caleb wrapped his arm around Harley's shoulders, his gaze glued to her face. "I'm not looking around the room, Ty," he corrected.

Harley smiled, and then reached up on tiptoe to kiss Caleb's cheek. He moved just in time to catch her lips with his. They kept the contact relatively short, but it was definitely more than a friendly kiss. Tyson caught a glimpse of their tongues as they touched briefly. It was more than enough to get Tyson's blood pumping. And enough to have a few folks nearby doing a double take.

"Y'all might want to take it easy on that," Tyson warned.

"Yeah. It's just hard being so close to her in that red dress that screams 'fuck me' and not taking her up on the invitation."

Harley gave them both a seductive grin. "Glad to know my evil plan is working."

"I'm going to make you pay for the teasing when we get home, darlin'. Give you that spanking you've been begging for."

She rolled her eyes, letting Caleb know his threat fell way short if he was trying to scare her with that so-called punishment.

"You want something to drink?" Caleb asked as he released Harley.

Harley nodded. "White wine."

Caleb looked at Tyson. "Beer?"

"Yeah. That sounds good. Thanks. In the meantime, I think I'm going to take our girl out there on the floor for a spin."

The fast line dance the deejay had played following their song was wrapping up, a slow one taking its place.

Tyson grasped Harley's hand and led her to the floor. She moved into his arms as if she'd been there forever. Sometimes it was hard for Tyson to remember that she'd only been back a little over a month, and that they'd only been together for four weeks. When he considered a lifetime of dancing and laughing and making music together and lounging on the couch, he couldn't believe how lucky he was.

Harley rested her head against his chest and they swayed slowly. Tyson saw Caleb chatting with Evan as they stood in line at the bar. His friend's eyes kept sweeping over to him and Harley, and he knew that Caleb was in just as deep.

Tyson still couldn't understand the lack of jealousy between them. Maybe he'd never figure that out. He also couldn't deny that the personal space between them was shrinking fast. At the beginning, Tyson was careful to avoid touching Caleb whenever they were in bed together with Harley. Given the close proximity, accidental brushes happened, but he'd been cognizant of it and had tried to keep his distance. Caleb had done the same.

Now that they were purposely *trying* to touch, it simply added to the magic that happened every time the three of them were in bed together.

Tyson couldn't deny there was something very hot about having his friend's hand on his ass as he took Harley, or the way he'd cupped his balls during that blowjob by the campfire. Goddammit—that touch alone had blown his mind.

As the song wound to a close, Tyson looked down just as Harley lifted her head. Their lips met and Tyson forgot about everything. Where they were. Who was looking on. Why they weren't supposed to kiss like this.

It all flew out of his head. The kiss lingered far too long to be anything other than what it was. The kiss of lovers.

When they broke apart, Harley gave him a look of instant regret. "Shit," she whispered. "Sorry."

"I don't think I am." Then he lifted his eyes, ready to assess the damage. Caleb's face was the first one he saw. His friend stood on the edge of the dance floor, his gaze locked on the two of them.

Before that moment, Tyson would have thought himself better able to read his best friend's thoughts. As he studied Caleb's blank expression, he felt completely blind.

"I think we've raised some curiosity," Harley whispered. Tyson forced himself to look away from Caleb to study the rest of the room.

Harley was right. More than a few people were looking in their direction. And the ones who weren't were looking at Caleb.

"Come on. Let's head back to the table." Tyson took her hand, guiding her back to their seats. Caleb met them there, placing their drinks on the table.

"How bad do you think it is?" Tyson asked quietly.

Caleb had kissed Harley beside the stage, in full view of more than a few people in the room. Now Tyson had taken his turn on the dance floor. While they hadn't been the center of attention, it was obvious by the sudden whispering behind hands that quite a few people had witnessed one or both kisses, and were now very curious about what the hell was going on. No doubt most folks were anticipating a fight between the best friends.

Boy, they were destined for disappointment there.

Before Caleb or Harley could reply, Macie claimed one of the empty chairs at the table. "Quite a show," she remarked with a grin.

Tyson grimaced. "You're not talking about the song we sang, are you?"

Macie laughed. "Good God, no."

Tyson figured if anyone had the lay of the land already, it was Macie. So he asked her the question he'd just posed to Harley and Caleb. "Give it to us straight. What's the damage?"

"You know that kids' game Telephone?" Macie asked.

Tyson and Harley nodded, while Caleb remained stone-faced.

"It's in full swing. And I'm pretty sure the jig is up. I mean, in all fairness, the question had already been posed around the bar a few times this past month. You three have been walking around with those big goofy grins, making mooneyes at each other nonstop. I've managed to deflect, brush it off as people reading too much into nothing. Usually I just say y'all missed Harley while she was gone. But when you add in Art going around telling everyone about Harley and Caleb kissing, and Phyllis Barton making comments about spotting Tyson and Harley in the park holding hands last week, the jig was pretty much up anyway. Half the crowd is looking at Luc, Diego and Jeannette, and thinking the Sparks' family has threesomes in their blood. The other half is anticipating you and Caleb fighting over Harley."

Caleb rubbed his forehead. "Jesus. Did *everyone* see us both kissing her tonight?"

Macie shrugged. "Not everyone. Just enough to get the ball rolling. Is this really a terrible thing?"

Tyson would have thought so a couple of weeks ago. Now he was sort of glad the cat was out of the bag. He was tired of hiding his feelings.

"I haven't talked to my folks," Caleb said quietly.

Tyson hadn't either. Both of them had been avoiding those uncomfortable confrontations. Honestly, Tyson suspected he would have spoken to his family already if they hadn't added that "other" factor to the mix. Coming out about the three-some would be tough, but admitting he was also bisexual and in love with Caleb as much as Harley was something else altogether. Mainly because he'd only just managed to admit that truth to himself.

Tyson glanced around the room until he found his parents' table. Both his mom and dad were looking in their direction.

"Cal," Tyson began. "I'm really fucking sorry, man."

Caleb reached out and put a hand on Tyson's shoulder. "It's past time, Ty. I know that. I'm not mad about any of this."

Tyson grinned. "Me either."

"So we'll just deal with it."

"Shit, this *really* isn't good," Harley muttered, her reaction taking Tyson by surprise. She'd been the one ready to scream about their relationship to the world.

"What? I thought you'd be happy that we—" Caleb started. However, one quick glance confirmed she wasn't looking at them. Rather, her attention was on something else.

"Shit," Tyson repeated as he and Caleb both stood. Art approached their table, his eyes gleaming with indignation.

Tyson had been surprised to see him at the wedding, until Sydney admitted she'd sent the invitations out months ago. She'd wanted to invite Polly, and at the time, sadly, that meant Art got to come too.

Obviously, the man had realized the wedding was a way to finally get to his estranged wife, but so far he'd kept his distance from Polly—probably taken aback by the fact she was sitting with her ex-husband. Art might be an asshole, but he wasn't stupid. Harley's dad had Art by at least seventy-five pounds—all of it muscle. And he wasn't exactly sending Art warm, fuzzy looks.

There was no doubt everyone had expected any wedding drama to stem from Art and John Mills. Not from Harley, Caleb and Tyson.

Art had to notice Caleb and Tyson flanking Harley, but he foolishly ignored them. "Certainly made a spectacle of yourself tonight, didn't you?"

Harley narrowed her eyes.

"Art," Caleb warned.

Art looked at Caleb with absolute disdain. "You'll burn in hell for this. All three of you will!"

The man's voice was loud and it carried in the room, despite the music playing. Tyson saw that most people had stopped dancing and talking. Every eye in the room appeared to be on them.

"This isn't the time, Art," Tyson said quietly, hoping the man would catch on, calm down. Tyson hated bringing all this tension to his cousin's wedding. Sydney and Chas didn't deserve to have their happy day ruined by the likes of Art.

While he didn't feel guilty about his feelings for Caleb and Harley, Tyson felt damn bad about dropping the bomb at Syd's reception.

"Not that I should be surprised," Art continued, his attention turned back to Harley. "You always were a slut. Just like your mother."

Caleb lunged forward, intent on doing serious bodily harm, but Harley reached out to stop him, her grip on his arm firm.

"No, Cal. Don't. He's not worth it."

Tyson's hands were clenched into fists as well; the only thing staying him was the thought of Sydney. He forced himself to breathe deeply, to calm down.

Before either of them could figure out the next move, Mr. Mills stepped up to the table, next to Art. "Apologize to my daughter."

Art scowled, his lips firmly pressed closed.

"*Now*," Mr. Mills said through gritted teeth.

Art barely looked at Harley as he muttered the least sincere "sorry" in history.

"You have ten seconds to get your sorry ass out of here or I'll remove you myself." John's voice was deep and deadly.

Art glanced up and visibly paled. "You stole my wife."

"No, Art. You lost her. It's time you accept that and move on."

Art's gaze traveled the circle and for the first time since he'd approached their table, he seemed to realize he was outnumbered. The last person he looked at was Polly, who'd come to stand next to Harley, her hand on her daughter's shoulder protectively.

"I'm done with you. I'll sign the papers on Monday." It was the last thing Art said before he turned and walked away from them all. No one spoke until he was completely out of the room.

Polly sank down into the chair next to Harley. "Are you okay?"

Harley nodded, looking somewhat amazed. "Yeah."

John walked around the table to claim the seat on Harley's other side and he reached for her hand. "If it hadn't been a wedding, I would have beat that asshole into the ground for calling you that."

"It's okay," Harley said, her smile growing. "Honest."

"No. It's not." Granddad pulled up another seat at the table as Macie rose.

"I'll leave y'all alone," she said. As she walked away, Macie gave Tyson and Caleb a pleased wink.

Tyson looked at Caleb, then Harley. "We'll give you all some privacy to talk."

John smiled at them gratefully and nodded, then turned his concerned attention back to his daughter.

As he and Caleb stepped away from the table, Tyson looked at his friend. "Wow. I wasn't expecting—"

"Neither was Harley. Look at her face. It's like she just won the lottery."

"Yeah." Tyson smiled, and then glanced around the room until he found Sydney and Chas, standing near the front table. "Give me a minute." He made a beeline for the bride and groom.

"Syd—" Tyson started.

Sydney took his hand before he could say more and placed a quick kiss on his cheek. "If I'd had to place a bet on which cousin would make a scene at my wedding, you would have been the bottom of the list."

"I'm so fucking sorry, Syd."

She gave him a funny look. "What? Why? That was nothing. Honey, this is Texas. A wedding without drama is a failed event. You made sure my wedding will be talked about for weeks, maybe months. Because, damn, Ty, that's some juicy stuff right there."

"You realize this isn't making me feel better."

Sydney laughed. "Sorry. Not sorry. I'm so happy for you. Caleb and Harley are the best."

"We didn't mean to spring it on you like this. Weddings are..."

"...the perfect place for romance," Sydney finished.

Chas shook Tyson's hand. "Stop worrying, Ty. It'll all work out in the end. Congrats, man."

Tyson watched the newlyweds return to the dance floor without a care in the world.

Caleb stepped next to him. "You've got an awesome family."

"I know," Ty said with a smile. "So what now?"

"I'm not leaving. I'm not hiding my face or acting ashamed of this."

Tyson raised his hand. "That's not what I was suggesting. I think we should regroup. Give Harley time to talk to her family and then—"

"Tyson."

He took a deep breath before turning to face the speaker. So much for regrouping. He caught a quick glimpse of Caleb's sympathetic look before Tyson spun to face his father.

"Dad."

His dad looked at Caleb. "You mind giving us a second, Caleb?"

Caleb shook his head. "Not at all. I'm going to go hang with Logan. Judge," Caleb said, bowing his head in respect.

His father acknowledged Caleb briefly, and then gestured toward a quiet spot near the exit.

Tyson followed. He was running out of steam. Fast.

Once they were out of earshot of others, Tyson began. "Dad, listen—"

"No, Tyson. I don't want to have this conversation here. It's your cousin's wedding. This isn't the time or place."

Tyson agreed completely. "You're right. It's not."

"Your mother has a headache, so we're going to head home now. I'd like you to stop by for breakfast tomorrow morning. We can talk there."

While Tyson understood this wasn't the place to say all

they needed to say, he also wasn't looking forward to a long, sleepless night worrying about his father's feelings on what he'd just witnessed. "Fine," he said at last.

Dad glanced around the room briefly and Tyson followed the look. His father watched Harley with her parents for a moment before looking toward Caleb. When his eyes returned to Tyson's face, his emotions were locked down tight. Tyson didn't have a clue what his dad was thinking.

"Eight a.m."

It was all his father said before walking back toward Mom. He helped her pull her shawl over her shoulders. Mom caught his eye and gave him a worried smile and a quick wink that told him exactly what he needed to know in regards to *her* feelings. His mother would always love him. No matter what.

Deep down, Tyson knew—or maybe he hoped—the same was true for his dad. He raised his hand to wave and his mother returned the gesture. Then his parents left.

Tyson remained rooted to the spot, trying to summon the energy to rejoin the party once more. There were too many eyes still pointed his direction, too many whispers and disapproving looks.

"Damn. Usually weddings are so boring."

Tyson looked over as Evan stepped next to him. He was grateful for his cousin's humor. And his company. "What can I say? I like to do my part to stir up the gossips in town."

Evan gave him a funny look. "Actually, you don't. You've walked a pretty straight line for most of your life. Valedictorian of your class in high school. College scholarship, medical school. Apart from occasionally sneaking a few beers at parties when you were a teenager, you've been the ideal that pretty much every parent in Maris has held up as the comparison. You've set the bar high for their kids."

Tyson winced. "Guess there won't be too many mom and dads looking at their kids tomorrow saying, 'Why can't you be more like Dr. Tyson Sparks?'"

Evan shrugged. "I don't know. I'm pretty sure I'll say that to Eryn someday. You're a successful, hard-working, decent person, Ty."

Tyson was touched. Evan thought the world of his young daughter. "Thanks, man."

"You realize this isn't that big a deal?"

"Yeah," Tyson said sarcastically. "I can tell that from the general shocked-to-within-an-inch-of-their-lives responses we've been getting tonight."

Evan chuckled. "I blame social media. Everybody thinks everybody else gives a shit about their opinions these days because they're so easy to share. It started with Facebook, but as more time passes, people are starting to say out loud the things they would have politely kept to themselves in the past."

"Which means, either way, they would have thought it. That doesn't change their feelings about it."

"You don't care what the Phyllis Bartons or Art Johnsons of the world think. So let's have it. What did the Judge say to you?"

Everyone in the family—as well as in Maris—referred to Tyson's dad as the Judge. Tyson always imagined the name being set apart in quotation marks.

"He said we'd talk about it tomorrow morning. He didn't want to ruin Sydney's wedding. Although…"

Tyson looked around for his cousin, still feeling terrible about the drama he'd unleashed on her special day.

Evan pointed to the dance floor. Sydney was swaying in her new husband's arms. The couple only had eyes for each other, the love they felt in that moment so beautiful to witness. "I'd say Syd's doing just fine."

As Tyson glanced around the room, he realized that—for the most part—everything had gone back to normal, now that the threat/promise of drama had passed. Apart from Phyllis and her cronies with their heads together, chatting a mile a minute and casting him dirty looks from time to time, everyone else had gone back to the celebration.

With Art gone and their conversation concluded, Harley's parents had taken to the dance floor, while her granddad snagged Harley for a spin. Harley's family appeared to have embraced the news just fine—as she had predicted. In all fairness, Tyson suspected her parents were just so happy to have found their way back to each other, and to have their daughter in their lives again, there was very little Harley could have said that would make them push her away.

The dance floor was actually crowded with couples. Most of his aunts and uncles were there, along with Coop, who'd claimed Macie as his partner. Luc, Diego and Jeannette were wrapped up in a cute three-person dance, laughing quietly. Tyson felt a twinge of jealousy, longing for the day when he, Caleb and Harley could feel comfortable enough to be so openly together and in love without provoking a scene.

Watching the other trio, he realized they were definitely closer to that day now than they'd been at the beginning of the night. While they hadn't meant to unleash the news the way they had, he was actually starting to feel glad it was out there. Now they could deal with the aftermath. In some ways, that seemed like an easier road after weeks of worrying about the fallout. The cat was out of the bag and, just as Macie had predicted, most of the local folks had expressed their shock or said, "I knew it," and then moved on.

Evan caught him looking at Luc and Diego. "So…you and Cal…"

"It's not like that." Tyson didn't add the word "yet," though he definitely thought it.

Evan shrugged. "Wouldn't matter to me if it was. Just wondered. Thought maybe I'd really been blind to something all these years."

"No." He'd suffered from that same blindness himself.

"No one's been blind to your feelings for Harley. Or Caleb's for her. Or hers for you two. That, cuz, has been written on the wall in flashing neon since high school."

"So I keep hearing. Macie said the same," Tyson muttered.

"I suspect the next few weeks are going to be rocky for you. People will most likely start choosing camps and giving you their two cents worth. If you need an ear…"

Tyson smiled at Evan. They were the only two male cousins in a sea of girls. As such, they'd grown up closer than brothers, mainly because they were seriously outnumbered. "I appreciate that."

"For what it's worth, I'm rooting for the three of you."

"Now I just have to hope my talk with Dad tomorrow goes as well."

Evan winced. "Yeah. Jeannette laid the foundation there for you, but I'm not sure the cement has dried yet. Hell, I'm not sure it ever would have dried for you. While Jeannette is his niece and he loves her dearly, you're his only son, and you're entering into a relationship with not just a woman, but another man as well. Don't envy you that conversation. The Judge is a tough guy to talk to on a good day."

"Tell me about it."

"You're going to have to give your parents time to come to grips with this. Let it soak in."

Tyson knew his cousin was right. "That makes sense. I mean, the truth of it is, the three of us struggled with it as well at the beginning. Lots of wrestling with should we, shouldn't we."

"We come from good stock," Evan said proudly. "I don't doubt for a second that once your parents, and the aunts and uncles have had time to consider it, to see how happy you are, and to remember how much they already love Harley and Caleb, they'll come around."

"You know, between you and the talk I had with Macie a couple weeks ago, I'm feeling a lot better. Something I didn't think could happen."

Evan shook his head, smiling. "Not going to complain about being lumped in with Macie. She's excellent company to be in, as far as I'm concerned. Pretty sure that girl saved my marriage."

"Really?"

"When Annie and I were struggling to conceive, Macie gave me some good advice. So good, in fact, we were pregnant with Eryn the next week."

"Please tell me you didn't take medical advice from Macie," Tyson said, wondering what on earth Macie could have said that would help a couple produce a baby.

Evan gestured toward the bar with a tilt of his head. "Let's go get a couple of beers and I'll tell you all about it."

* * *

LOGAN PLACED a comforting hand on Caleb's shoulder when he joined him at the table. Lacy was sitting a couple tables away with her cousins Adele and Gia, no doubt discussing the bomb he, Tyson and Harley had just dropped in the middle of the reception.

"Hey, man. I just want to say I'm happy for the three of you."

Caleb grinned, something he hadn't anticipated doing for the rest of the evening. Logan was one of his closest friends. And with one comment, he'd lifted the tiniest piece of anxiety off his shoulders. "Thanks, Logan. That means a lot. Sorry to spring it on you like this. We should have told you."

Logan gave him a funny look. "What are you talking about? Believe me, Cal, this turn of events is no surprise to anyone who knows the three of you."

"I find that damn hard to believe, even though Tyson said Macie made the same comment. Threesomes are hardly commonplace occurrences."

"Fine. I'll reword it. If anyone was made for a long-term happily ever after created with three people instead of two, it was you guys."

"Guess it took us a while to figure that out for ourselves."

Logan shrugged. "Timing is everything. Look at me and Lacy. I never really saw myself falling for Evan's kid sister, never imagined that the little girl in pigtails who constantly followed us around, begging to be included in our games, would be the woman of my dreams. Life takes us on some strange, winding roads, but at some point we all eventually get where we were meant to be."

"Strange, huh? That's a pretty good description."

"The three of you have been focused on other things for so long. Tyson spent years working his way through medical school, then building his practice. Harley dedicated half her life to caring for Johnnie. And you, as the only son to Maris' version of the Rockefellers, were damn busy too. I'm just glad y'all finally looked around and caught sight of each other."

"Me too."

Logan paused, as if trying to decide something. Then he went for it. "You and Ty…that's happening too, right?"

If anyone would have seen anything in all the years they'd been friends, it would have been Logan. Caleb didn't reply at first, but he needed someone to talk to. And he trusted Logan. Loved him like a brother. "It hasn't. Not yet."

"Yet," Logan repeated, latching onto the pivotal word.

"Is that something else you've always suspected?" Caleb found that impossible to believe. Mainly because he'd never suspected it himself. Still wasn't sure where these feelings for Tyson were coming from. They felt new. Brand spanking new. And not like something he'd repressed for twenty years.

Logan shook his head. "No. Not at all. But, well, it just seems right, you know?"

Caleb blew out a long breath. "It does?"

"Yeah. And don't ask me how I know that, I just do. You want deep introspection and analysis, you're going to have to look somewhere else. I'm a lot better at expressing myself through the furniture I make. Ask me to put something in words, and you're asking for disaster."

"Not sure how to explain all this to my parents. Hard enough admitting to the threesome. These feelings for Tyson…"

"You're a good guy, Cal. Always have been. Always will be. You fell in love with your best friends. And they're in love with you. If you really think about that, you'll realize that doesn't make you a bad person. Makes you a lucky son of a bitch."

"Shit. You're right. It does."

Logan chuckled and slapped him on the back. Lacy joined them at the table and gave Caleb a quick kiss on the cheek. "Damn, that was a hell of a show," she teased.

"Lacy," Logan warned, though there was no heat in his voice. "Poor guy's feeling guilty enough as it is."

Lacy laughed. "Oh yeah, like you weren't just giving him shit."

Logan shook his head. "Actually, you came back before I could get a few digs in. Sort of stole my thunder."

Caleb let them have their fun. After all, he'd just spent the past few months making fun of his friend for being so ridiculously smitten. Now, as he glanced out at the dance floor at Harley, twirling around in her granddad's arms, he felt a bit lovestruck as well. And since the night had already gone to hell in a handbasket, he might as well go for broke.

"Excuse me, please." Caleb rose and walked toward Harley, who had her back to him. Granddad saw him coming and grinned.

"Mind if I cut in?" Caleb asked.

Her granddad released her as Harley moved into Caleb's arms. Neither of them started moving. Instead, Caleb looked at the older man, who simply said, "It's about time."

Caleb laughed as her grandfather left the floor.

Harley's face told him everything he needed to know about her feelings. He suspected he was the only thing keeping her rooted to the ground. She was flying high, elated.

"Guess the talk with your family went well."

"Did you see how they came over to me? How they stood up for me?"

Caleb nodded and marveled at the irony of the evening. He and Tyson had never doubted their parents. Never questioned their love or their support. The same hadn't held true for Harley. Not in a very long time.

"I saw. It was great."

"It was freaking awesome. I wish..." Her words faded as her eyes dimmed just a bit. Caleb was becoming used to that look. Knew it meant she was thinking of her brother.

"Johnnie saw it. He knows."

"You're right. He does. Apparently, Mom and Dad both made their peace with Johnnie before he died. I was so angry at them for so long, I was too blind to see things that were happening right in front of me. My mother stopped by the house quite a bit those last few months before he passed away. They took walks and talked. I always assumed she was whining to him about her husband, giving Johnnie the same 'poor me' routine I got, even though he looked forward to her visits. She admitted they spent a lot of time talking about me. Johnnie gave her advice on how to mend the fence. God, we all wasted so many years."

"So you'll make up for lost time. They were okay with..." He let her fill in the blank.

She nodded. "Dad was already on board, and he either filled Mom and Granddad in before tonight or they just figured it out. Either way, they said they're happy if I'm happy."

The smile on her face lit up the entire room. Then she tilted her head and placed her hand on his cheek. "I'm sure your parents will be okay too." He lifted one shoulder, not feeling her confidence. When she added "eventually," he realized she knew his battle wouldn't be so easily won.

"Yeah. At least Tyson's parents won't be blindsided when he goes to talk to them. They know what's coming. Dad didn't feel up to the wedding today, so they're snug as bugs in their bed, sleeping, blissfully unaware of what's coming their way tomorrow."

Harley laughed and rolled her eyes. "Jesus, Cal, you're not one of the Seven Horsemen of the Apocalypse, riding in with a plague. Just say the words. We should have said something right from the outset. You guys have spent the better part of a month worrying about this until it feels so big, it seems impossible."

He pulled her close, holding her tighter. "You're right. That's exactly what we've done."

"I know it's not the easiest path, but there's no other way for us to go. You know that, right?"

"I don't want another way, angel. I want *this*. You, me and Tyson. Tomorrow, I'll come clean. I'm finished pretending I'm not completely in love with you, Harley Mills."

She lifted her face and Caleb gave in to the pull. He kissed her.

When they parted, Tyson was standing nearby.

"How would you guys feel about bouncing early?" he asked.

Caleb nodded. "Let's go."

They said their goodbyes then rode home in relative silence. For the first time since embarking on their romance, they crawled into bed, sex the furthest thing from their minds.

Harley wrapped her arm around Caleb's chest, her leg tossed over his. Tyson spooned her from behind, his hand resting on Caleb's waist. The three of them lay quietly, Caleb's thoughts consumed with the coming confrontation with his dad.

"It's going to be okay," Harley said at last.

"I know," Caleb said. "As long as I have you two, we're going to be just fine." As he said the words, he realized they were the truth.

He was exactly where he belonged.

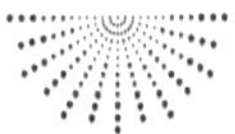

CHAPTER TWELVE

Caleb sat at the counter at Sparks Barbeque the next morning, staring at his cup of coffee. He'd spent a wakeful night, working out what he'd say to his dad. Finally, he gave up on pretending to be asleep when his restlessness kept disturbing Tyson and Harley.

He'd crawled out of bed, showered and came here for caffeine. The Feed and Seed opened in an hour, but his dad would be getting there right about now. Sunday morning was typically slow business-wise, as most folks were in church. They could talk without interruption.

Which meant it was time for Caleb to pay the bill and the piper.

He was just about to ask Adele for the check when someone claimed the stool next to him. Caleb glanced over, surprised to see his dad.

He should have fucking known better than to delay his visit.

As always, the news in Maris had managed to travel faster

than the speed of light. His parents hadn't attended the wedding. But that didn't mean they didn't know every single thing that happened.

A fact made more obvious when his dad asked, "Want to tell me something, Caleb?"

"How did you hear?"

"Phyllis Barton was ringing your mother's phone at six a.m. this morning. The woman has no boundaries."

Caleb grimaced. "Should have expected that."

Dad cut straight to the chase. "How long has it been going on?"

"Since Harley got back to Maris." Actually, his heart had been lost in the barn after Johnnie died, but his dad didn't need all the nitty-gritty details.

"How long is it going to last?"

Caleb didn't hesitate to reply. "Forever."

Dad winced. "Caleb, this kind of thing…well…I'm not sure forever is in the cards."

"You're wrong."

"No, I'm not. It's illegal. And unnatural. And the hell of it is, once it's over, your reputation is going to be sullied beyond repair."

Caleb shook his head. Before he could say more, his dad went for the jugular. "Your mother's worried."

"I'm thirty-two years old, Dad. I know my heart. I know what I want."

"And you think that's Harley *and* Tyson? I don't even understand how that works. Are you gay?"

"No." Caleb was starting to suspect he was actually bi, but this conversation was bad enough without throwing that into the mix. Despite his frustration with his dad's reaction, the man actually wasn't reacting any differently than Caleb had expected. He'd known this talk would suck. Dad wasn't disappointing him there.

"I'm not sure you've considered all the ramifications of your actions."

"Actually, I have. And I'm sorry, Dad. But I can't walk away from something that makes me this happy."

"You're endangering everything we've worked for, Caleb. Our businesses, our livelihood, our standing in the community."

"I'm not living my life based on other people's opinions."

"What about your mother and me? Do our feelings about this count for anything?"

Caleb sighed. "I love both of you very much. You know that. And I'm sorry this is hurting you. But I'm not walking away from Harley and Tyson and what we have together. If you care about me, you won't ask me to do that."

"What does Judge Sparks have to say about this?"

Caleb shrugged. "I don't know. Tyson is talking to him this morning."

"I can't imagine he'll condone this."

"It doesn't matter if he does or not."

Dad looked as if Caleb had struck him. "I didn't raise you to act like this."

"Like what, Dad? A free thinker? A risk taker? My own man? Sorry to break it to you, but that's *exactly* how you raised me. You don't answer to anyone, either."

His father was a leader in the community because he wasn't afraid to speak his mind, to stand up for his beliefs.

Dad rubbed his eyes wearily. When he spoke again, his voice was tired, less aggressive. "What do you expect me to say about this, Cal?"

"You don't have to agree with me. I actually know you won't. But can you give me time to show you why it works? Can you respect my feelings enough to step aside, but not walk away?"

His father fell silent for a long time. Caleb didn't seek to fill it with more words. He'd said all he needed to say. The ball was in his dad's court.

"I need some time to think about this," Dad said at last. "Why don't you take this week off?"

Caleb swallowed heavily. "Just this week?"

Dad hesitated, and then nodded slowly. "Yeah. Just this week."

"And then?"

"Come over to the house for lunch on Thursday. We can talk more then. I just need…"

"Time," Caleb repeated.

His dad nodded as he stood and walked away without saying goodbye.

The conversation hadn't gone well, but in truth, Caleb had imagined much worse.

He ordered another cup of coffee and sat there as the restaurant slowly filled up, more and more people stopping in for Sunday breakfast.

"Looks like your morning's been as shitty as mine," Tyson said, sinking down on the stool next to Caleb with a heavy sigh. Adele had a coffee cup in front of Tyson, filled with the hot brew, in under thirty seconds. She offered both of them a sympathetic smile, and then she simply walked away to let them talk.

"No advice from one of your cousins?" Caleb said as Adele moved away. "Man, we must look like a couple of sad sacks."

Tyson chuckled. "I went to see my dad this morning."

"Mine left a little while ago. How'd it go?"

"Surprisingly okay. I think Jeannette's relationship with Luc and Diego actually helped my case. Dad's not as easy to shock these days."

Caleb snorted. "That's good. Meanwhile, my pop is reeling. And apparently my mother is fretting."

"Everything we expected? You out of the will? Disowned?"

Caleb shook his head. "No. I'm not sure, but even as upset as my dad was, I think he was trying to understand it. He loves you and he loves Harley. He always has. If it had been two strangers, maybe he would have flipped his lid, lost his shit. As it is, I think deep down he'll get it. Eventually. Even if he doesn't want to come out and admit that."

"That's funny. That's what my dad said. Almost exactly. Said I'm his son and he loves me and nothing I could do would ever change that. Then he said if I was going to go off the deep end and do something insane like fall in love with two people, at least I had enough common sense to pick people worthy of that emotion."

Caleb chuckled. "Damn. That's pretty cool of him."

"Yeah. Dad's pretty cool. And your dad will come around too. He's just going to be a tougher nut to crack. Which we knew."

"We did. I'm going to lunch on Thursday to talk to him and Mom together."

"Think it would help if I went with you?"

Caleb considered that, appreciating the offer. "I'm not sure. Let me think about that and I'll let you know."

"You think he's hesitant to embrace this relationship because he's worried about business?"

"I'm sure that's part of it. He prides himself on his role as a leader around here. He's probably as worried about *his* reputation as mine."

But Caleb had faith in his father. Despite his straight-and-narrow ways, his dad valued his family above everything. Caleb clung to the idea that somehow, somewhere down the road his dad would come around.

"So we did it," Tyson said.

"And no one died."

"And the town didn't burn down."

"And no meteor struck the planet."

They chuckled.

"Any regrets?" Tyson asked.

Caleb shook his head. "Only that we took so long to do it."

Tyson laughed. "Jesus, man. It's only been a month. So what's next?"

Caleb knew exactly what Tyson was asking. While they'd been okay with touching in the dark, that was where it ended. In the harsh light of day, there had been no discussing it. Hell, they'd barely acknowledged it. It was like they left it all in the bedroom and pretended it hadn't happened.

"I think it's time we piss or get off the pot."

Tyson rolled his eyes. "Never get tired of your crude, yet accurate observations. You're okay with..." Tyson waved his hand between them.

"Yeah. I am. You?"

"Yeah."

"So, we're taking it up a notch?" Caleb asked, realizing that if a female had been involved in this conversation there would have been at least seventy-two thousand more words. He and Tyson didn't need to beat the dead horse. The writing had been on the wall for weeks.

"I think we are."

"Where's Harley?"

"I left her in bed."

Caleb grinned. "Let's go home."

"Race you there."

HARLEY HADN'T MEANT to sleep in so late, but it was rare to get the king-size bed all to herself. After Caleb and Tyson had gone out to talk to their fathers, she'd intended to get up and make herself an early breakfast.

Then she'd rolled over and slept the sleep of the dead for another two hours. Something she never did.

She almost felt guilty about being so relaxed and peaceful, considering what Tyson and Caleb were going through this morning. But after so many years of nonstop family drama, everything that happened last night felt like a dream. One she didn't want to wake up from.

So she didn't.

"Seriously?"

She opened her eyes and grinned when she found Caleb and Tyson standing in the doorway. She'd heard them come in, but sheer blissful laziness kept her in bed. Besides, why leave the bed when she preferred them joining her there?

She sat up. "How did it go?"

Caleb stripped off his shirt and then his pants. "We'll talk after."

"Just tell me if it was good or bad."

Tyson shrugged as he took off his own clothes, reclaiming the spot he'd abandoned a couple hours earlier. "Both."

That told her nothing. And everything. They'd expected Tyson's dad to take things okay, given the fact Jeannette had already blazed the threesome trail in the Sparks' family. And they'd known Caleb's dad would *not* take it well. So basically everything they'd anticipated had come to pass.

She glanced at Caleb, studying his face. He was smiling at her, his eyes unclouded by the anxiety that had been there since last night.

"You're okay?"

He nodded. "I love you, Harley. Nothing on earth is going to change that."

She smiled and fell into his open arms. Harley placed her lips on his, intending to give him a comforting kiss, but that idea was quickly swept away when Caleb pressed her lips open, his tongue touching hers.

The kiss turned molten in seconds. Tyson, never one to be left behind, cupped her breasts, kneading the sensitive flesh in the way she loved, the way that never failed to set her aflame.

There was something different about them. Something freer. Easier.

She pulled away a few inches from Caleb and twisted, creating a circle, rather than remaining a physical barrier between them.

"Kiss," she whispered, making it clear she didn't plan to be a part of it.

Neither man hesitated. One second they were facing each

other, the next their lips were connected, taking each other boldly, passionately.

"Holy shit," she murmured. They broke apart to look at her.

"Harley—" Tyson began.

"I get it now. Watching the two of you…"

Caleb grinned as he reached for her. He kissed her, and then turned his face back to Tyson. Then Tyson kissed her. It was hot, sensual. So much more than Harley could have imagined.

"Need you," she gasped, when Caleb gave her the briefest moment to suck in a breath of air.

"Want you," Tyson almost growled. His hand slid around her waist until he found her ass. Twisting, he pulled her over him. He stroked her ass before giving her one quick, hard spank.

"Hey!" she said in surprise.

"Caleb promised you a spanking last night."

Harley narrowed her eyes, and then decided to take matters into her own hands. She reached out, gripping each man's dick in one of her palms. Stroking them firmly, she tilted her head, seductively, letting them know she was more than adept at distraction. "Are you sure you wouldn't rather do something else first?"

Tyson looked at Caleb. "She's really fucking good at that," he said through gritted teeth.

Caleb chuckled. "No kidding. I'm not stopping her. We'll just spank her longer later."

She continued to stroke their dicks as Tyson and Caleb leaned closer to each other, kissing once more. The three of them had slept together—had sex—nearly every single night for the last month. Yet, this time felt like the first time.

The best time.

Tyson gripped her wrist and pulled her hand away from his cock so he could twist her. Once again, she was in the middle, Tyson at her back. His erection rubbed against her ass, while Caleb's bumped against her stomach. Both men were hard, ready to go.

She turned her face and kissed Tyson as Caleb bent and sucked one of her nipples into his mouth firmly.

"God, more."

She needed friction. And pounding. And she needed it now.

Caleb lay back on the mattress, pulling Harley on top of him. She wasted no time, lifting her hips as Caleb placed his cock at her pussy. They both groaned in pleasure as she slid down, taking him fully inside her.

Tyson knelt behind her, his fingers stroking the place where they were joined.

"Jesus," Caleb muttered. "That feels so good."

Harley bent down to kiss Caleb, her breasts pressed against his chest. She was surprised when he wrapped his arms around her and tightened his grip.

"I can't move," she said.

"Tyson," Caleb said, not loosening his hold on her. "Come here."

Tyson moved to their side as Caleb reached for the pillows, propping his head up. Harley figured out his intent in a moment and she was delighted. She grasped Tyson's cock and pulled it toward her and Caleb's waiting mouths.

Together, they licked and stroked his erection, taking time

to suck him in. Their own lips continued to meet and touch as well. As far as sexy kisses went, Harley was fairly certain they'd just created the world's greatest one.

Tyson's fingers curled in her hair, tugging it until her scalp stung. The pain morphed into pleasure that had her pussy muscles clenching against Caleb's dick.

Caleb grunted. "Pull harder, Ty."

Tyson pressed his cock deeper into her mouth as Caleb tilted his hips, moving in even farther. Harley was on sensation overload, but given the muttered curses and soft moans from her lovers, it was safe to say she wasn't alone.

She was almost there, when suddenly Tyson retreated, his cock escaping her lips with a pop.

"Ty!" she said, trying to draw him back to her.

"No, Harley. Not this time."

She didn't understand what he meant until he reached toward the bedside table, pulling out a tube of lubrication. Suddenly, she knew exactly what they wanted—and she was ready. So freaking ready.

"Yes," she hissed when Caleb resumed his grip on her, holding her body tight against his.

"Hold still, angel," he murmured when she jerked at the first touch of the cold lube against her ass.

She closed her eyes, forcing herself to suck in some deep breaths. She was equal parts excited and terrified. Her emotions must have shown.

"Harley, look at me," Caleb said, lifting her chin to bring her face up. "If it hurts, say so and we stop. If you hate it, say so and we stop. Okay?"

"I want this," she said, afraid they were misinterpreting her reaction.

Tyson leaned over and kissed her bare shoulder. "I know, beauty. But remember what Caleb said anyway."

"Okay," she whispered as she rested her cheek on Caleb's chest, listening to the steady thumping of his heart.

Tyson took his time getting them ready for this. She lost count of how many times he added more lubrication to her ass as he stretched her with one finger, then two, then three. Each time he added another digit, Caleb grunted.

"I can feel everything you're doing to her," he finally admitted. "It's unbelievable."

By the time Tyson was up to three fingers, Harley was in a frenzy. Her skin shimmered with heat and electricity. Every part of her felt too over stimulated for touch. And yet, that's exactly what she was begging for.

"Please, Ty," she cried out hoarsely. She'd been making the same plea for nearly ten minutes, but Tyson wasn't going to rush things, wasn't going to run any risk of hurting her.

Finally, he slowly withdrew his fingers, replacing them with the head of his cock. It was a tighter fit. She'd expected that.

"Breathe," Caleb whispered in her ear.

She managed one deep gasp before Tyson pressed in a bit farther and all the air escaped in a loud exhale.

Caleb's arms tightened around her, and she realized he was as affected as she was. He'd said he could feel it all.

She tried to press back, tried to drive more of Tyson inside when he went too slow, but Caleb's grip was iron-clad.

"Don't move." His words were deep, dangerous. Sexy.

"But—"

Tyson placed a hard slap against her ass. "Do what he says, Harley."

Slowly, he made his way inside, and Harley felt like crying tears of relief when he reached the hilt.

"Okay?" Caleb asked.

She nodded, not bothering to lift her head from his chest. "More," she demanded.

Harley expected them to laugh at her haughty tone, but both men seemed spellbound by her desire.

"Baby," Tyson soothed. "Take a minute to adjust. I think—"

"Move now," she said louder. "Right now. And, Tyson, I swear to God, if you keep up that snail-like pace, I'll cut your dick off in your sleep."

That did produce a chuckle. From Caleb. "You heard our girl, Ty. Apparently you're not doing it right. Hurry up."

Harley opened her eyes in time to catch the dirty look Tyson threw in Caleb's direction. "I'll remember that when it's *your* ass I'm fucking."

Harley's pussy clenched at the thought, something both men felt.

At that point, none of them were capable of holding back, of denying themselves exactly what they wanted.

Tyson began thrusting in and out of her ass shallowly as she and Caleb started a very gentle rocking motion. It only took a few minutes for all hell to break loose as they turned into ravenous beasts.

Caleb guided Harley up and down with strong hands on her waist. Tyson gripped her hips, pulling her toward his cock faster.

"Jesus!" Tyson yelled out, his climax striking hard. He came inside her, jets of hot come filling her ass.

Harley was mere seconds behind him, and her orgasm

took Caleb down as well, her inner muscles clenching tightly, milking his dick, squeezing out every drop of come.

Harley collapsed on top of Caleb, a lifeless heap. It was several minutes before she realized he wasn't any more alive. He lay motionless beneath her, only the rise and fall of his chest reassuring her he hadn't perished in the bliss.

Tyson caged the two of them as he held himself upright on his hands and knees.

His dick, now soft, was still tucked inside her. They were both still inside.

"I think I died," she joked when she found enough breath to speak.

Caleb snorted once. "So did I."

Tyson didn't reply. Instead, he slowly slid out as she shuddered, then dropped next to her on the mattress.

"What the fuck *was* that?" he muttered, his voice rife with amazement.

"There's not a single word in the English vocabulary that will describe that," Harley murmured.

"Not sure there's a word to describe any of this." Caleb looked over at Tyson, and Harley grinned when they leaned toward each other to steal a quick kiss. What a difference twenty-four hours could make.

Yesterday, they were still dating in secret, and Tyson and Caleb were avoiding a very obvious truth about themselves.

Today, every single piece had fallen into place.

"So what's the plan?" she asked with a sleepy grin.

"It's Sunday," Tyson reminded her.

Harley laughed. "We're letting the spirit move us again?"

"Yep," Caleb confirmed.

"Any idea if it's going to move either of you to the kitchen?" she asked. "I'm starving."

Her words woke up something in Tyson as his stomach growled. "Bacon?"

Caleb's dick stirred briefly, growing hard again.

Harley lifted her head, shaking it. "Yep. Just what you said, Ty. A strong wind or the smell of bacon. Let's go eat."

Macie leaned on the counter, her chin resting in her palms. Tyson, Harley and Caleb were sitting in a corner booth, talking and laughing about something. They were so in love it oozed out of them.

She sighed.

"What's wrong, darlin'?" Coop asked from his usual spot at the bar.

She shrugged. "Nothing."

He looked over his shoulder to determine what she was looking at. "You're not happy about Tyson's new relationship?"

She glanced back at Coop and grimaced. Lately it was getting harder and harder to hide stuff from the man. He was really good at reading her thoughts. "Don't be silly. I think it's great."

He grinned at her. "Yeah. I can tell by the heavy sighs and sad face you're real pleased."

She rolled her eyes. "It's not them. It's what they represent."

"And what's that?"

"Love...a relationship. Something that's going to last forever."

"And that's a bad thing?"

She shook her head. "Of course not."

"I see. So you're jealous."

She snorted, but didn't bother to deny it.

"You want that?"

She looked him dead in the eye, somewhat surprised he would ask. Why *wouldn't* she want that? "Of course I do."

"Good."

"Good?" Macie asked, thinking that was a very strange answer.

"Yeah. Good."

She blew her bangs up with a hard breath and crossed her arms. So much for getting any sympathy or helpful advice from Coop. "You wanna know something, Hank Cooper?"

He shook his head. "Not really, but I'm sure you'll tell me anyway."

"You're weird."

Coop laughed off her description—and then did something that very few people were capable of when he said, "And you're beautiful."

He rendered Macie Sparks speechless.

ARE you ready to see Macie find her happily ever after? Be sure to grab Waiting for Love, available now.

And be sure to check out other books in the Sparks in Texas series.
Waiting for Us (prequel)

Waiting for You
Waiting for Her
Waiting for Him
Waiting for Them
Waiting for Love
Waiting for Snow

ABOUT THE AUTHOR

Virginia native Mari Carr is a New York Times and USA TODAY bestseller of contemporary romance novels. With over two million copies of her books sold, Mari was the winner of the Romance Writers of America's Passionate Plume award for her novella, Erotic Research. She has over a hundred published works, including her popular Wild Irish and Compass books, along with the Trinity Masters series she writes with Lila Dubois.

Follow Mari:
www.maricarr.com
mari@maricarr.com

Join her newsletter so you don't miss new releases and for exclusive subscriber-only content.

www.ingramcontent.com/pod-product-compliance
Lightning Source LLC
Chambersburg PA
CBHW031235210726
48287CB00003B/788